CAPTURED BY PIRATES

JUSTINE & RON FONTES

ILLUSTRATED BY DAVID WITT

GRAPHIC UNIVERSE · MINNEAPOLIS

Story by Justine and Ron Fontes

Pencils and inks by David Witt

Coloring by Hi-Fi Design

Lettering by Bill Hauser

Graphic Universe
A division of Lerner Publishing Group, Inc.
241 First Avenue North
Minneapolis, MN 55401 U.S.A.

Website address: www.lernerbooks.com

Library of Congress Cataloging-in-Publication Data

Fontes, Ron.
        Captured by pirates / by Ron Fontes and Justine Fontes ; illustrations by David Witt.
          p.   cm.——(Twisted journeys)
        ISBN: 978–0–8225–6201–6 (lib. bdg. : alk. paper)
        1. Graphic novels. I. Fontes, Justine. II. Witt, David. III. Title.
        PN6727.F675C36 2007
        741.5'973——dc22   2006101599

Manufactured in the United States of America
4 5 6 7 8 9 – DP – 13 12 11 10 09 08

ARE YOU READY FOR YOUR *Twisted Journeys®?*

YOU ARE THE HERO OF THE BOOK YOU'RE ABOUT TO READ. YOUR JOURNEYS WILL BE PACKED WITH ADVENTURES ON THE HIGH SEAS. AND EVERY STORY STARS *YOU!*

EACH PAGE TELLS WHAT HAPPENS TO *YOU* AS YOU SAIL THE OCEAN BLUE AND MEET A BAND OF NASTY PIRATES. *YOUR* WORDS AND THOUGHTS ARE SHOWN IN THE *YELLOW BALLOONS.* AND YOU GET TO DECIDE WHAT HAPPENS NEXT. JUST FOLLOW THE NOTE AT THE BOTTOM OF EACH PAGE UNTIL YOU REACH A *Twisted Journeys®* PAGE. THEN MAKE THE CHOICE *YOU* LIKE BEST.

BUT BE CAREFUL...THE WRONG CHOICE COULD MAKE YOUR PIRATING DAYS VERY SHORT!

Salt spray whips hair into your eyes. You strain to see past the waving arms of the other passengers. You're leaving London on a cold, spring day in 1635. You clutch your violin, afraid your heart might burst with excitement over your first ocean voyage.

Father tucks his gold watch back into his vest. "How do you feel, child?"

For the past two months, since Mother died, you've felt like crying. But you try to keep a stiff upper lip. Feeling the ocean roll under the swift ship shakes your heart loose. You are too excited to be sad. "Do you think we will see any pirates, Father?"

He chuckles, then puts his large hand on your shoulder. "If I thought so, you would not be here."

GO ON TO THE NEXT PAGE.

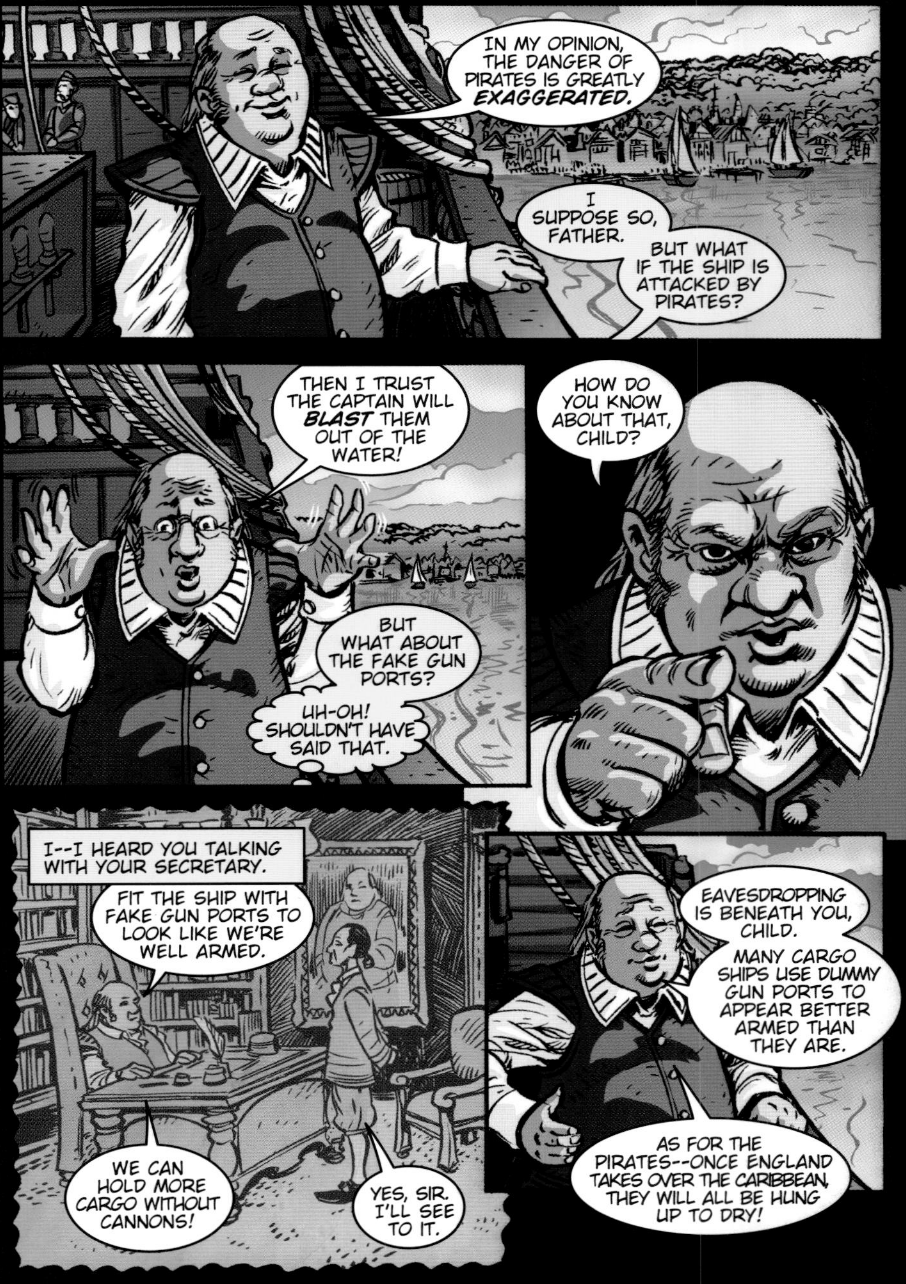
IN MY OPINION, THE DANGER OF PIRATES IS GREATLY **EXAGGERATED.**
I SUPPOSE SO, FATHER.
BUT WHAT IF THE SHIP IS ATTACKED BY PIRATES?
THEN I TRUST THE CAPTAIN WILL **BLAST** THEM OUT OF THE WATER!
BUT WHAT ABOUT THE FAKE GUN PORTS?
UH-OH! SHOULDN'T HAVE SAID THAT.
HOW DO YOU KNOW ABOUT THAT, CHILD?
I--I HEARD YOU TALKING WITH YOUR SECRETARY.
FIT THE SHIP WITH FAKE GUN PORTS TO LOOK LIKE WE'RE WELL ARMED.
WE CAN HOLD MORE CARGO WITHOUT CANNONS!
YES, SIR. I'LL SEE TO IT.
EAVESDROPPING IS BENEATH YOU, CHILD.
MANY CARGO SHIPS USE DUMMY GUN PORTS TO APPEAR BETTER ARMED THAN THEY ARE.
AS FOR THE PIRATES--ONCE ENGLAND TAKES OVER THE CARIBBEAN, THEY WILL ALL BE HUNG UP TO DRY!

GO ON TO THE NEXT PAGE.

YOU'RE PROUD TO BE ENGLISH. SPAIN HAS RULED THE NEW WORLD LONG ENOUGH.

FATHER'S COMPANY IS ONE OF THE FIRST TO SET UP A TRADING POST ON THE ENGLISH ISLAND OF BARBADOS. OTHERS ARE SURE TO FOLLOW.

AFTER ALL, THE ENGLISH NAVY HAS DEFEATED THE SPANISH *FOUR TIMES!*

LET'S GET SETTLED IN THE CABIN.

PERHAPS YOU CAN REST OR PLAY THE VIOLIN UNTIL TEATIME.

YOU'VE ENJOYED THE VIOLIN LATELY. WHEN MOTHER WAS ALIVE, YOU BEGGED TO QUIT.

NOW THAT SHE'S GONE, THE VIOLIN SEEMS YOUR ONLY WAY TO BE WITH HER.

6

GO ON TO THE NEXT PAGE.

You play until your fingers ache and your stomach growls. The smell of fresh baking leads you to the galley. The cook invites you into the cramped room and hands you a steaming scone.

Something small and furry moves just past your vision. You almost scream!

The cook chuckles. "Just a cat, child! Not a rat, though there are plenty of those in the hold. That's why we keep the cats."

You try to regain your composure and take a bite of the scone. "Thank you. It's delicious!"

The cook smiles. "It's better than the hard tack you'd get on a navy ship, that's for certain." Then he reaches out a calloused hand to you. "My name is Sandbourne, but everyone calls me Sandy."

You tell Sandy your name. He asks you about the violin and persuades you to "give him a tune." Sandy likes your music, especially Mother's lull-a-bye.

GO ON TO THE NEXT PAGE.

When you stop playing, you still hear music. You realize the sound is coming from below decks. You take your
leave of Sandy and follow the music to the crowded
quarters of the common sailors.

In the dank, wooden gloom, a red-haired sailor plays
the fife. Two of his friends tap on drums. Other sailors
sing and dance.

The redhead puts down his fife to address you. "Will
you join us?"

You know Father wouldn't approve of you spending
time with common sailors. But the music is lively and
you long for friendship.

8   GO ON TO THE NEXT PAGE.

WILL YOU...

...resist the temptation of low company and hurry back to the cabin?

TURN TO PAGE 77.

...play along with the sailors' tune?

TURN TO PAGE 86.

The buccaneers have more to say. They offer two of the *Endeavour*'s longboats to any mutineers who don't want to join Jack's band.

"You risked your lives for your freedom," Smoky Jack tells the grumbling sailors. "And you've been kind enough to give us the loot, so let us part as fellow Brethren of the Coast."

The mutineers immediately start to argue about which way to go. Squid wants to go north. Templeton is sure that traveling south will keep the rebels safe from the hangman's noose. Finally, they decide to split up.

TURN TO PAGE 16.

SHARING FOOD HELPS YOU MAKE FRIENDS WITH THE COMMON SAILORS. ONE DAY, YOU ASK IF ANY OF THEM HAS EVER SEEN A MERMAID.

HERE ARE THE *SCARS* FROM THE TIME I ALMOST DID.

BACK WHEN I WAS IN THE NAVY...

MY FRIEND SUDDENLY SHOUTED, "MERMAID!" I LOOKED UP AND SAID, "IT'S JUST A PORPOISE."

WE WERE NOT ALLOWED TO SPEAK ON DECK. MY FRIEND AND I WERE BOTH *FLOGGED*.

WAS IT COMPLETELY AWFUL?

FLOGGING'S BROKEN MANY GOOD MEN.

I LEFT THE NAVY, BUT I CAN'T SEEM TO LEAVE THE SEA.

AS SMITTY SPEAKS, YOU ARE SHOCKED TO SEE HIGGINS SWIPE SOME CREAM.

TURN TO PAGE 67.

11

WILL YOU. . .

. . .rush for the nearest tree, even though it's a tough climb?

TURN TO PAGE 15.

. . .run to the tree with the buzzing beehive, even though it's farther away?

TURN TO PAGE 19.

. . .run as fast as you can?

TURN TO PAGE 81.

The chubby Irish trumpeter joins in, and so does the tall, skinny African drummer. Several of the pirates, including Captain Jack, jump up and dance a jig. At the end of the song, they all cheer!

You make friends with the trumpeter called Gabby, short for Gabriel.

"After the trumpeter who plays at the end of the world," the Irishman explains with a wink. "I've practically forgotten my real name. Everyone just calls him Drums."

The African nods. Back in his homeland, Drums was also a musician. You've never met anyone from Africa before. But when you play music together, it feels like you're old friends.

GO ON TO THE NEXT PAGE.

Gabby and Drums tell you to make the best of things.

You want to ask Smoky Jack to keep his promise to go back for Father. But your new friends advise you not to push the pirate captain.

"He's nice enough, as captains go," Gabby says. "But you don't want to make him angry. You're better off praying for your father's soul. Don't expect to see him again in this lifetime."

You become used to the idea of making music on the pirate island. Instead of joining in raids, you, Gabby, and Drums open a music store. You sell handmade instruments and even give music lessons. To earn extra money, you play at parties.

Over time, you create a new sound that combines English music with Caribbean. But the tunes you write are filled with your sadness over not finding some way to save Father.

THE END

THE SPANISH HAVE LONG USED MASTIFFS TO SCARE THE NATIVES. NOW THE DOGS ROAM HISPANIOLA IN *WILD PACKS*.

NOOOO! HELP!

WOOF!

WOOF!

WOOF!

FEAR HELPS YOU CLIMB LIKE A CAT.

WOOF!

WOOF!

WOOF!

THE HUNGRY HOUNDS MAKE A SHORT MEAL OF ANDERSON.

THEN THEY RETREAT INTO THE JUNGLE.

YOU PUT ON THE HAT AND RETRIEVE THE SHOVEL. BUT YOU CANNOT FIND THE NERVE TO DIG FOR THE TREASURE.

WHO WILL WATCH MY BACK? WHO CAN BE TRUSTED WHEN IT COMES TO TREASURE?

AND HOW CAN I POSSIBLY HOPE TO AVOID THE *CURSE?*

THE END

Your choice has gotten much more complicated!

WILL YOU. . .

...go north in Squid's longboat?
TURN TO PAGE 58.

...go south in Templeton's longboat?
TURN TO PAGE 68.

...sign the articles to join Captain Jack's crew?
TURN TO PAGE 71.

...stay with Father and the passengers, promising ransom to the pirates?
TURN TO PAGE 103.

With your hostage for a shield, you grab a blunderbuss. You plan to use the heavy shotgun to hijack the sloop and rescue Father. But the buccaneers rush you! You can't scare pirates with a threat. You must shoot someone—or die!

You level the weighty weapon on the closest pirate and squeeze the trigger...

The blunderbuss misfires. Pain and blood replace your hand.

Pirates shout. Someone calls for Chips, the carpenter. The surgeon was "boarded by the grim reaper" on a recent raid and hasn't yet been replaced. So the carpenter will have to do. His tools are pretty much the same.

Shock dims your vision. Voices swirl.

"Kill the brat for breaking the promise!"

"Put the poor thing out of its misery."

Chips leans close. "If I cut off your hand and cauterize the wound, you might live."

TURN TO PAGE 72.

17

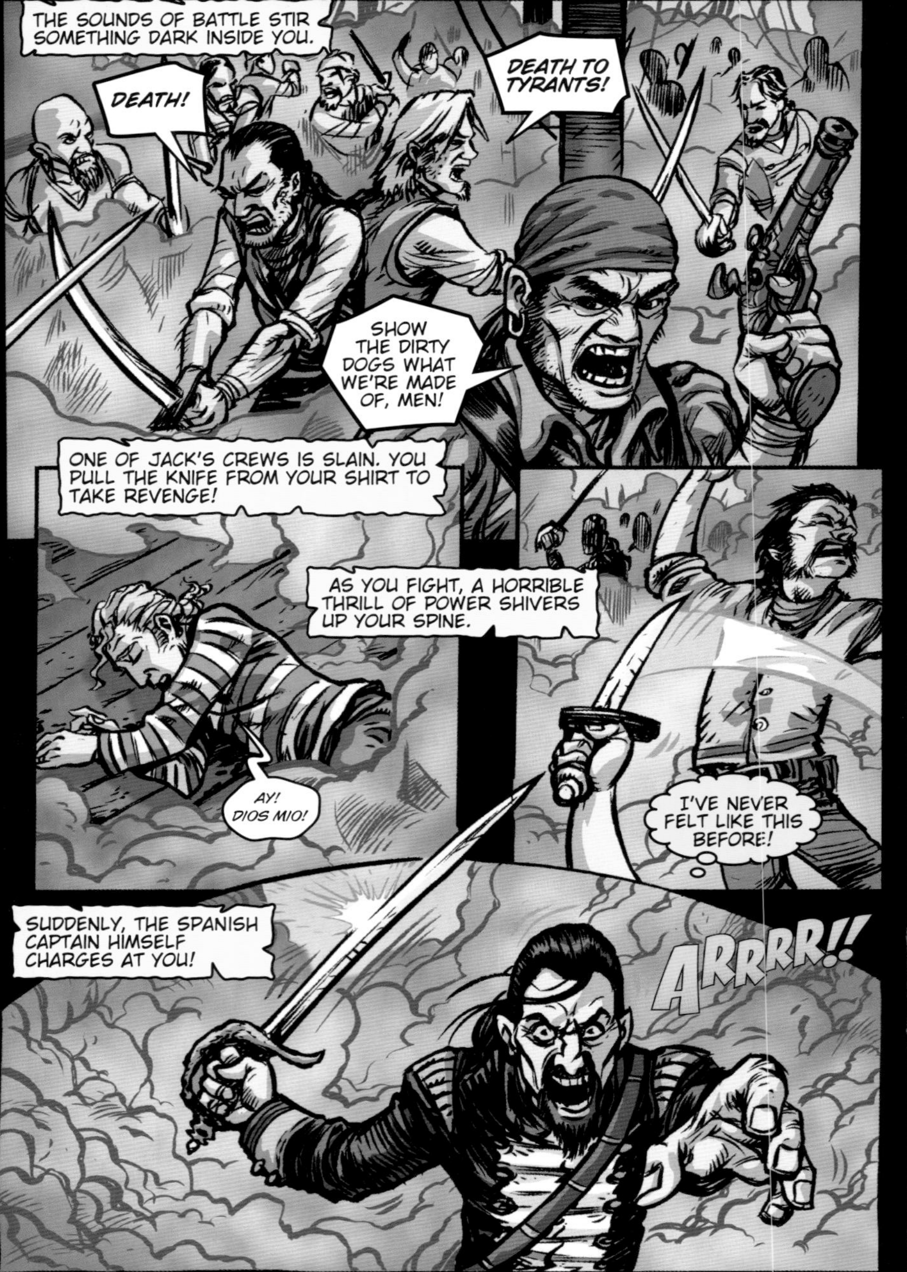
THE SOUNDS OF BATTLE STIR SOMETHING DARK INSIDE YOU.
DEATH!
DEATH TO TYRANTS!
SHOW THE DIRTY DOGS WHAT WE'RE MADE OF, MEN!
ONE OF JACK'S CREWS IS SLAIN. YOU PULL THE KNIFE FROM YOUR SHIRT TO TAKE REVENGE!
AS YOU FIGHT, A HORRIBLE THRILL OF POWER SHIVERS UP YOUR SPINE.
AY! DIOS MIO!
I'VE NEVER FELT LIKE THIS BEFORE!
SUDDENLY, THE SPANISH CAPTAIN HIMSELF CHARGES AT YOU!
ARRRR!!

TURN TO PAGE 30.

You scramble up the tree just
in time to escape the large, hungry dogs.
But Anderson isn't as lucky.

The old man freezes in panic, then tries to run. The
dogs tackle him in seconds. Their sharp teeth snap
onto his limbs. Anderson looks up at you in a frantic
plea for help.

You break off a branch and slam it against the hum-
ming hive. Angry bees swarm out! You fling your arms
over your head to cover your face.

The yips and whines of unhappy hounds fill your ears.
Then the barks grow distant as the dogs flee back into
the jungle.

GO ON TO THE NEXT PAGE.

You uncover your face and see Anderson. "You saved my life!" He's bumpy with bee stings but glad to be alive. And somehow the ordeal seems to have cleared his mind.

You take turns standing guard and digging for the treasure. THUNK! Your shovel finally hits metal. The small chest is so heavy with gold, the two of you can barely lift it. You and Anderson will be rich for the rest of your lives.

Washed, shaved, and back in civilization, Anderson proves to be a great friend. He helps you raise an expedition to find Father. Months later, you trace him to an Arawak village. To your sorrow, you learn that he died of malaria not long ago.

But before his death, Father had married an Arawak woman and had a son. You bring your half-brother home to England. You teach him how to play the violin. And when he's old enough, you sail together back to his homeland, where you build a school in Father's honor.

THE END

TWISTED JOURNEYS®

WILL YOU. . .

...stick it out with Captain Dandy?
TURN TO PAGE 78.

...make a desperate escape attempt
using empty wine casks?
TURN TO PAGE 85.

The cat pounces and the parrot shrieks! All around you, groggy pirates grab their weapons with deadly quick reflexes.

Gabby rubs his red eyes and blinks just in time to see Stripes deliver the killing bite right under your hammock. The trumpeter also sees that you did nothing to help.

"Of all the scurvy..." Gabby chases Stripes away from her prey. But there is nothing he can do for Rosy. "She's dead!" Gabby exclaims. Then he turns his angry eyes on you. "And so are you!" The fat pirate lunges. His chubby fingers crush your throat.

"Don't kill the musicker!" someone shouts.

"At least hold a trial," Portuguese Peg adds.

GO ON TO THE NEXT PAGE.

YOU FIND OUT THE HARD WAY THAT PIRATES ENJOY STAGING MOCK TRIALS.

THE LOOKOUT CALLED HAWK IS YOUR DEFENSE ATTORNEY.

THERE'S NO CRIME HERE-- UNLESS YOU WANT TO CHARGE THE CAT.

THE FIDDLER WAS WIDE AWAKE! I SAW!

WE INTEND TO PROVE THAT THE DEFENDANT COULD HAVE SAVED ROSY BUT DID NOT.

CAN'T WE JUST HANG THE CHILD AND GET ON WITH BREAKFAST?

SUDDENLY, THE ONE-LEGGED COOK MOUNTS HIS OWN DEFENSE.

THE FIDDLER'S ME FRIEND! ANY THAT WANTS A HANGING MUST GO THROUGH ME!

NOT EVEN GABBY IS KEEN ENOUGH ON YOUR DEATH TO FACE PEG'S PISTOLS. THE TRIAL IS OVER.

GO ON TO THE NEXT PAGE.

But you have made an enemy. The tubby trumpeter gossips against you. By the end of breakfast, Captain Jack's band is bitterly divided. Some hate the new musicker. The rest "don't give a drowned rat what happened to the noisy bird."

Seeking peace among his men, Captain Jack makes a suggestion. The crew should vote on whether to keep you in their group or trade you to another, he says. Before you quite realize what is happening, you have been exchanged for a bottle of fine brandy. Your new master is a well-dressed pirate known as Captain Dandy.

GO ON TO THE NEXT PAGE.

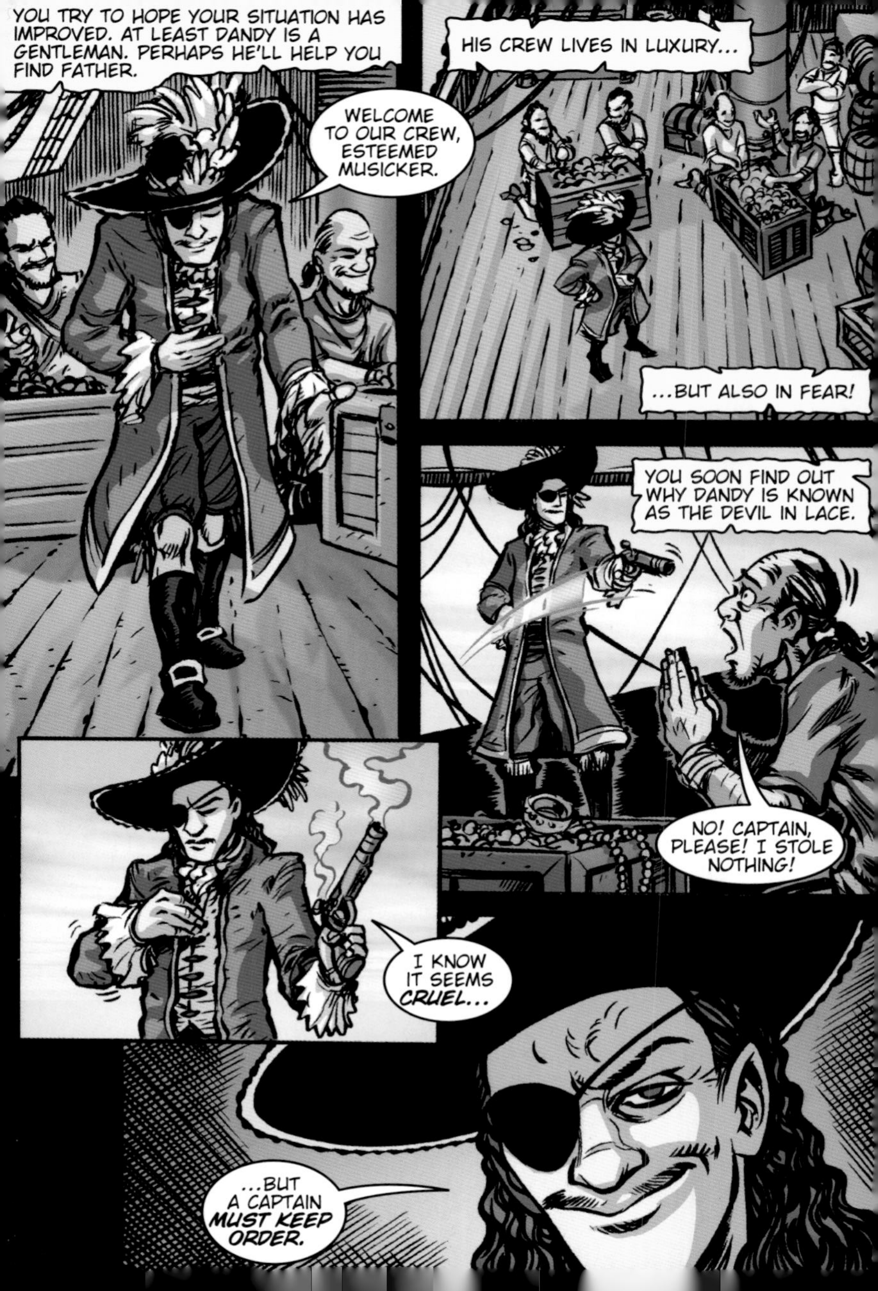
YOU TRY TO HOPE YOUR SITUATION HAS IMPROVED. AT LEAST DANDY IS A GENTLEMAN. PERHAPS HE'LL HELP YOU FIND FATHER.
WELCOME TO OUR CREW, ESTEEMED MUSICKER.
HIS CREW LIVES IN LUXURY...
...BUT ALSO IN FEAR!
YOU SOON FIND OUT WHY DANDY IS KNOWN AS THE DEVIL IN LACE.
NO! CAPTAIN, PLEASE! I STOLE NOTHING!
I KNOW IT SEEMS *CRUEL...*
...BUT A CAPTAIN *MUST KEEP ORDER.*

WILL YOU...

...become Captain Jack's musicker?

TURN TO PAGE 73.

...declare that you'd rather die with Father?

TURN TO PAGE 83.

The deranged pirate tells you his name is Anderson. You wonder how he got the map and how he came to this state of mind. But he insists there's no time to waste. Now that you're here to watch his back, the treasure will be his at last!

After a short hike, you come to a clearing with a strange group of rocks. Your spine tingles as you compare the stones to the map.

"This is the place!" Anderson exclaims.

He starts to dig but keeps turning around to look over his shoulder. "Are you watching my back?" the pirate demands.

A buzzing sound makes you jump. But it's just a few bees flying into their hive, which hangs from a low branch a few trees away.

Suddenly, Rosy squawks! The parrot stares into a mass of green leaves. Glowing eyes peer at you from among them. You hear one low growl answered by another.

TURN TO PAGE 12.

Each day, the *Endeavour*'s fresh food supplies dwindle—except at the captain's table. You take an apple and remember to hide it from the sailors. But as you're strolling the deck, the apple falls out of your pocket!

"What's this?" exclaims Squid.

"Might have known they'd be eatin' like kings above decks," adds Templeton.

You retrieve the apple as quickly as you can. But the sailors' bitterness lingers in your ears.

That night at the captain's table, you watch pear juice drip off Father's double chin. "Why can't the sailors have fruit, too?" you ask

"There isn't room to carry enough fruit for everyone," Captain Timothy explains.

"We must have space for cargo," Father adds.

During the night, you are jolted awake by the CRACK of lightning. It strikes one of the *Endeavour*'s masts. The ship sinks in a sudden storm.

GO ON TO THE NEXT PAGE.

YOU WAKE UP IN A LONGBOAT.

ARE YOU HUNGRY, CHILD?

WE MANAGED TO SAVE SOME FOOD. WANT SOME?

YES, PLEASE!

SORRY, OLD CHAP.

NOT ENOUGH TO GO AROUND.

YOU ARE STARVING! BUT *THIRST* IS EVEN WORSE THAN HUNGER.

YOU FALL INTO A DELIRIUM.

YOU KNOW YOU SHOULDN'T DRINK SALT WATER, BUT YOU CAN'T STOP YOURSELF.

SO . . . THIRSTY. . .

WHEN YOU DIE, SQUID AND TEMPLETON CUT UP YOUR CORPSE FOR BAIT. AND THE CYCLE OF LIFE CONTINUES-- WITHOUT YOU.

THE END

The Spanish captain is about to run you through!

WILL YOU. . .

...duck?
TURN TO PAGE 40.

...climb up the rigging?
GO TO PAGE 97.

You corner Father for a serious talk. "What if those meat traders really were buccaneers?" you ask. "What if they saw the fake gun ports?"

You expect Father to once again dismiss your fears and perhaps scold you for your nosiness. Instead, he bursts into tears!

"I'm all at sea, child! I don't know what to believe anymore," Father begins. "Last night, your mother came to me in a dream. She said, 'Take my babe home. Leave the sea to the sailors.'"

You blink back tears at the mention of Mother.

"As you know, I do not believe in ghosts and other nonsense," Father declares. "But just now outside the cabin, I felt her presence again as a chill warning. I shall tell the captain to turn about at once. We'll make some excuse, but you will be home by the time the daisies bloom."

You are, but you always wonder what would have happened if you have seen the journey through.

THE END

You have no way of finding the island on your own, so you sneak up to Smoky Jack's navigator. You press the knife to his throat with one hand and cover his mouth with your other. Despite your complete terror, you whisper in your deepest, toughest voice, "Make a sound and I'll kill you!"

You get the navigator to a longboat and order him to row to the island where Father was marooned.

SPLASH! You turn and see a porpoise. Before you can turn back, an oar smashes into your skull.

You awaken back in Jack's camp. Your limbs are bound. Angry voices discuss different ways to make you pay for your broken promise.

Then the navigator suggests, "It's a pretty day for a sail—and a long walk off a short plank."

THE END

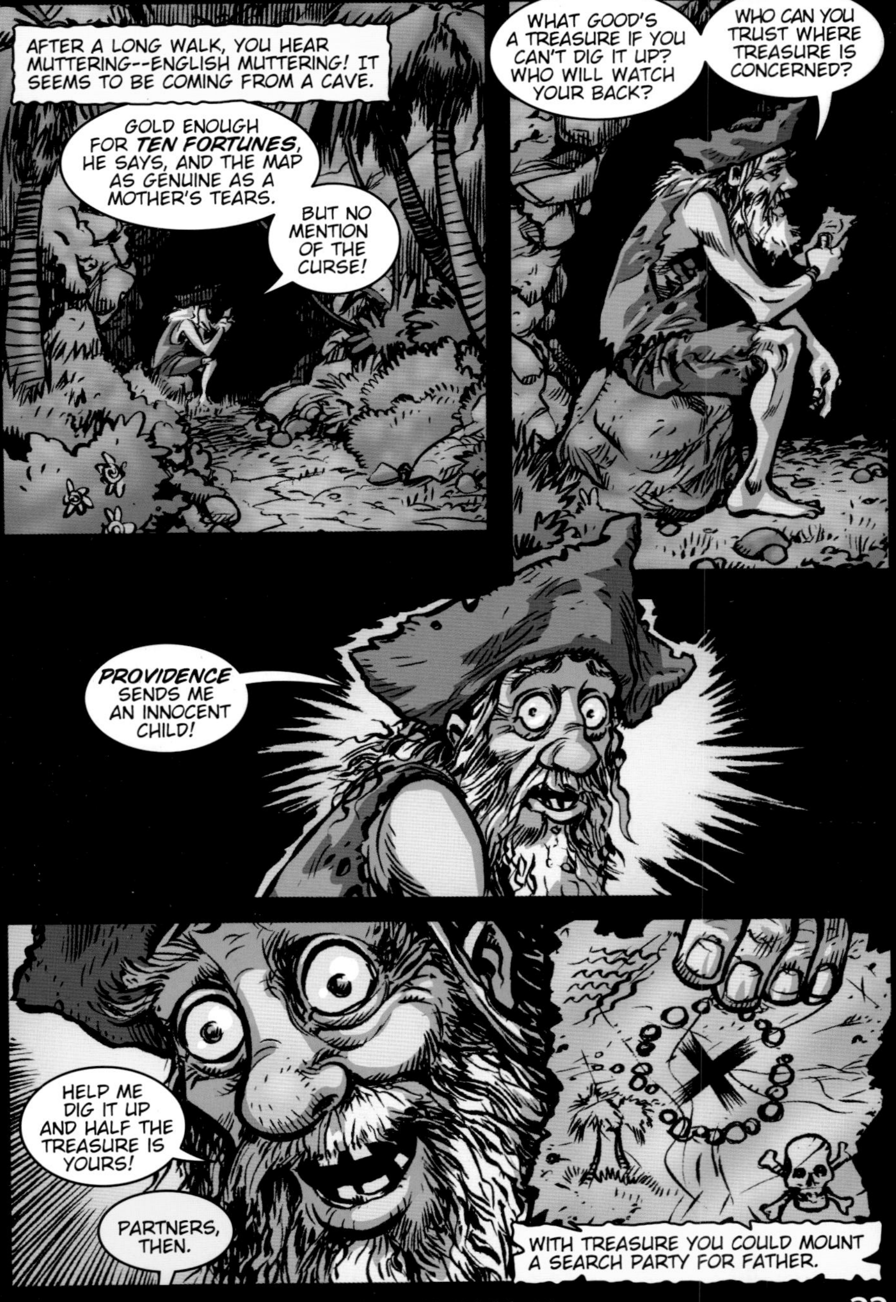

AFTER A LONG WALK, YOU HEAR MUTTERING--ENGLISH MUTTERING! IT SEEMS TO BE COMING FROM A CAVE.
GOLD ENOUGH FOR TEN FORTUNES, HE SAYS, AND THE MAP AS GENUINE AS A MOTHER'S TEARS.
BUT NO MENTION OF THE CURSE!
WHAT GOOD'S A TREASURE IF YOU CAN'T DIG IT UP? WHO WILL WATCH YOUR BACK?
WHO CAN YOU TRUST WHERE TREASURE IS CONCERNED?
PROVIDENCE SENDS ME AN INNOCENT CHILD!
HELP ME DIG IT UP AND HALF THE TREASURE IS YOURS!
PARTNERS, THEN.
WITH TREASURE YOU COULD MOUNT A SEARCH PARTY FOR FATHER.

TURN TO PAGE 27.

After just a few bites of the disgusting stew, the thought of Father robs you of your appetite. "Father must be very hungry by now, too," you mutter. You wonder if he is worse than hungry, if he's hurt or even...

You suddenly realize that Captain Jack has joined the group. "If you won't eat, then play, musicker! Let us hear what you can do!"

You know you should play a lively tune, like the ones the trumpeter and drummer have been playing. But you feel so sad and worried.

TURN TO PAGE 41.

You are determined not to join the fight.
Then you see Captain Jack. He's about to
be killed by the Spanish captain!

WILL YOU . . .

. . . change your mind, throw your knife,
and shout a warning to Jack?

TURN TO PAGE 46.

. . . sneeze?

TURN TO PAGE 75.

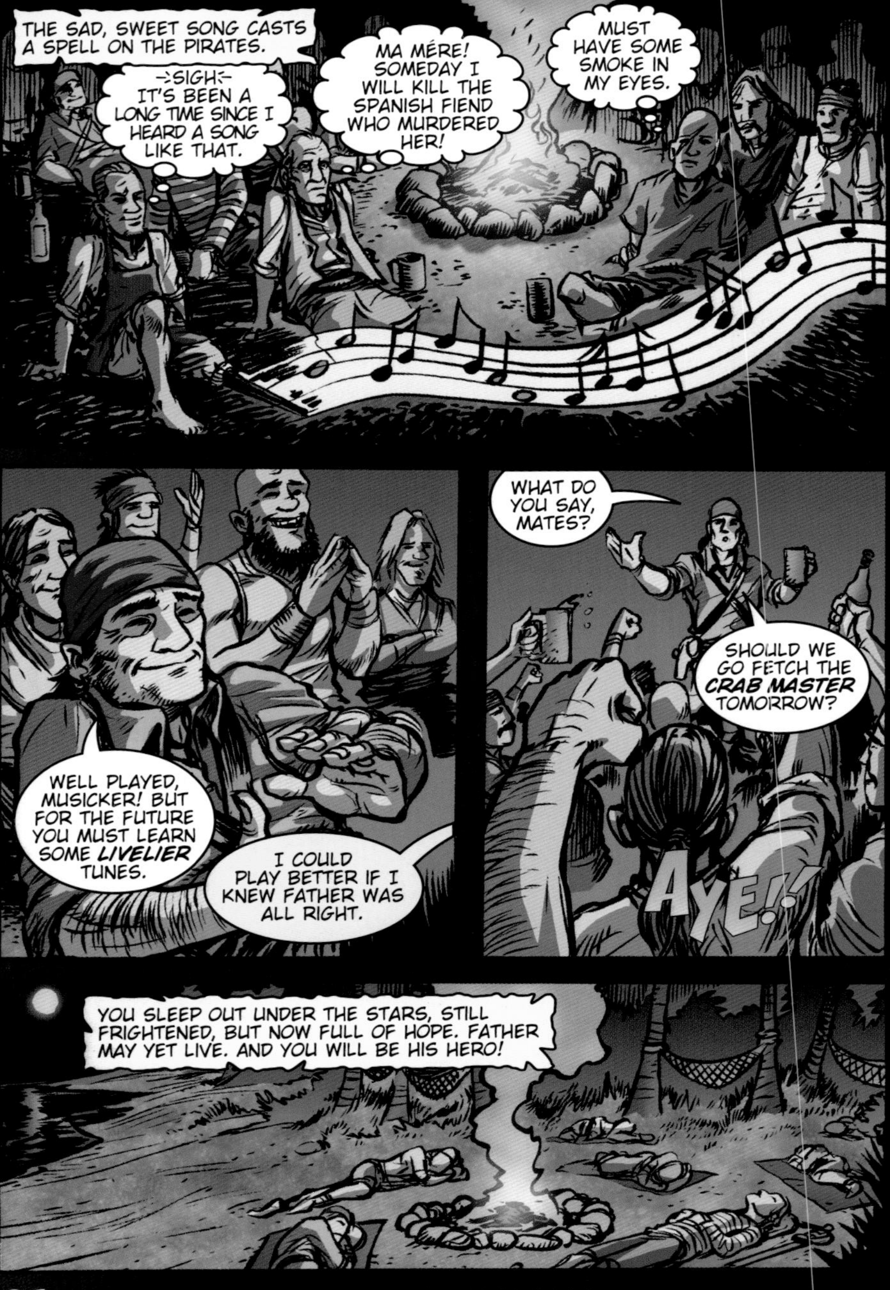
THE SAD, SWEET SONG CASTS A SPELL ON THE PIRATES.
⊰SIGH⊱ IT'S BEEN A LONG TIME SINCE I HEARD A SONG LIKE THAT.
MA MÉRE! SOMEDAY I WILL KILL THE SPANISH FIEND WHO MURDERED HER!
MUST HAVE SOME SMOKE IN MY EYES.
WELL PLAYED, MUSICKER! BUT FOR THE FUTURE YOU MUST LEARN SOME *LIVELIER* TUNES.
I COULD PLAY BETTER IF I KNEW FATHER WAS ALL RIGHT.
WHAT DO YOU SAY, MATES?
SHOULD WE GO FETCH THE ***CRAB MASTER*** TOMORROW?
AYE!!
YOU SLEEP OUT UNDER THE STARS, STILL FRIGHTENED, BUT NOW FULL OF HOPE. FATHER MAY YET LIVE. AND YOU WILL BE HIS HERO!

Insects buzz and bite all around you. You twist and turn in your unfamiliar hammock. Who ever heard of sleeping on strings? You slap at the bugs, but they just keep coming.

Finally, the peg-legged cook assigned to guard you hands you a gourd filled with fat. "Here, child. Smear this hog grease on your skin. I'll put some more leaves on the fire to make it smokier."

You thank the pirate and ask his name. "They call me Portuguese Peg," he says.

You cannot believe you are glad to have pig fat on your face, but the native insect repellant works. You fall into a deep sleep but have a horrible nightmare about Father walking the plank!

TURN TO PAGE 42.

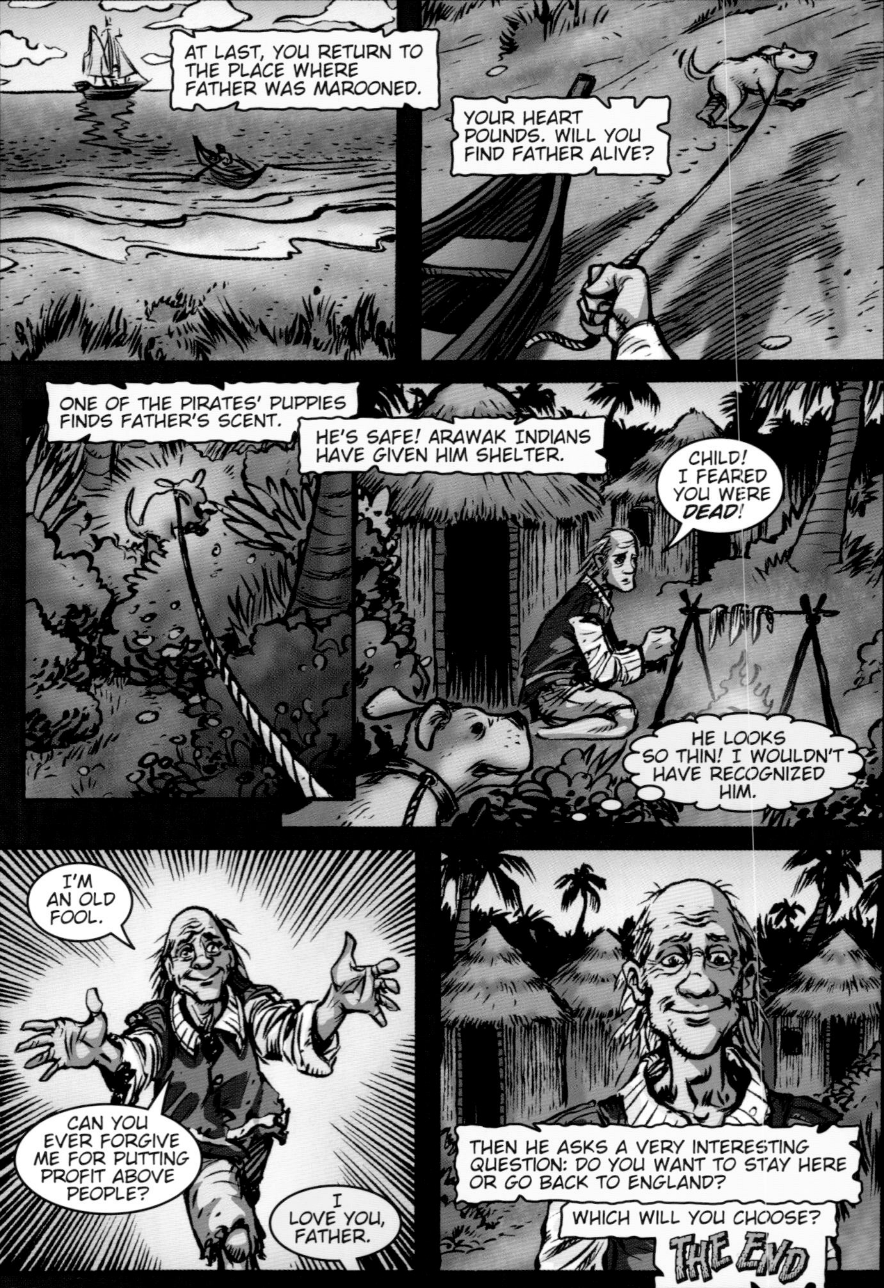
AT LAST, YOU RETURN TO THE PLACE WHERE FATHER WAS MAROONED.
YOUR HEART POUNDS. WILL YOU FIND FATHER ALIVE?
ONE OF THE PIRATES' PUPPIES FINDS FATHER'S SCENT.
HE'S SAFE! ARAWAK INDIANS HAVE GIVEN HIM SHELTER.
CHILD! I FEARED YOU WERE DEAD!
HE LOOKS SO THIN! I WOULDN'T HAVE RECOGNIZED HIM.
I'M AN OLD FOOL.
CAN YOU EVER FORGIVE ME FOR PUTTING PROFIT ABOVE PEOPLE?
I LOVE YOU, FATHER.
THEN HE ASKS A VERY INTERESTING QUESTION: DO YOU WANT TO STAY HERE OR GO BACK TO ENGLAND?
WHICH WILL YOU CHOOSE?
THE END

When Captain Jack calls for music, you try to play the violin. But you're so hungry, your hands shake. You burst into tears. The pirates are disgusted.

"What's the matter, did the silver spoon get stuck in your throat?"

"Let's put the spoiled puppy out of its misery," someone suggests.

The next thing you hear is the POP of a pistol. You wonder why the sky is suddenly farther away as you fall to the ground, never to hunger again in this lifetime.

THE END

Missing you by inches, the Spaniard's sword gets stuck in the rigging. Before he can pull it free, Captain Jack deals a death blow. The Spaniards soon surrender.

The pirates shout, "Three cheers for Fiddles!" "Hurrah for our lucky musicker!" They want you to join them and take a share of their biggest raid yet.

They even rescue Father. You barely recognize the thin, tan, humble man you find on the island. "I prayed for forgiveness," Father says. "And my prayers were answered! Let us give the rest of our lives to serving God."

As Father describes his plans for a quiet life, the pirates' offer becomes more and more appealing. You sign the articles. Your share of the treasure is enough to send Father back to England.

During the next raid, a Spanish cannonball rips the sloop's hull. Despite Father's distant prayers, you're torn to bits by flying splinters.

THE END

TWISTED JOURNEYS®

WILL YOU . . .

. . . play the only sea shanty you know, as loud and lively as you can?

TURN TO PAGE 13.

. . . play the song that's in your heavy heart, Mother's lull-a-bye?

TURN TO PAGE 36.

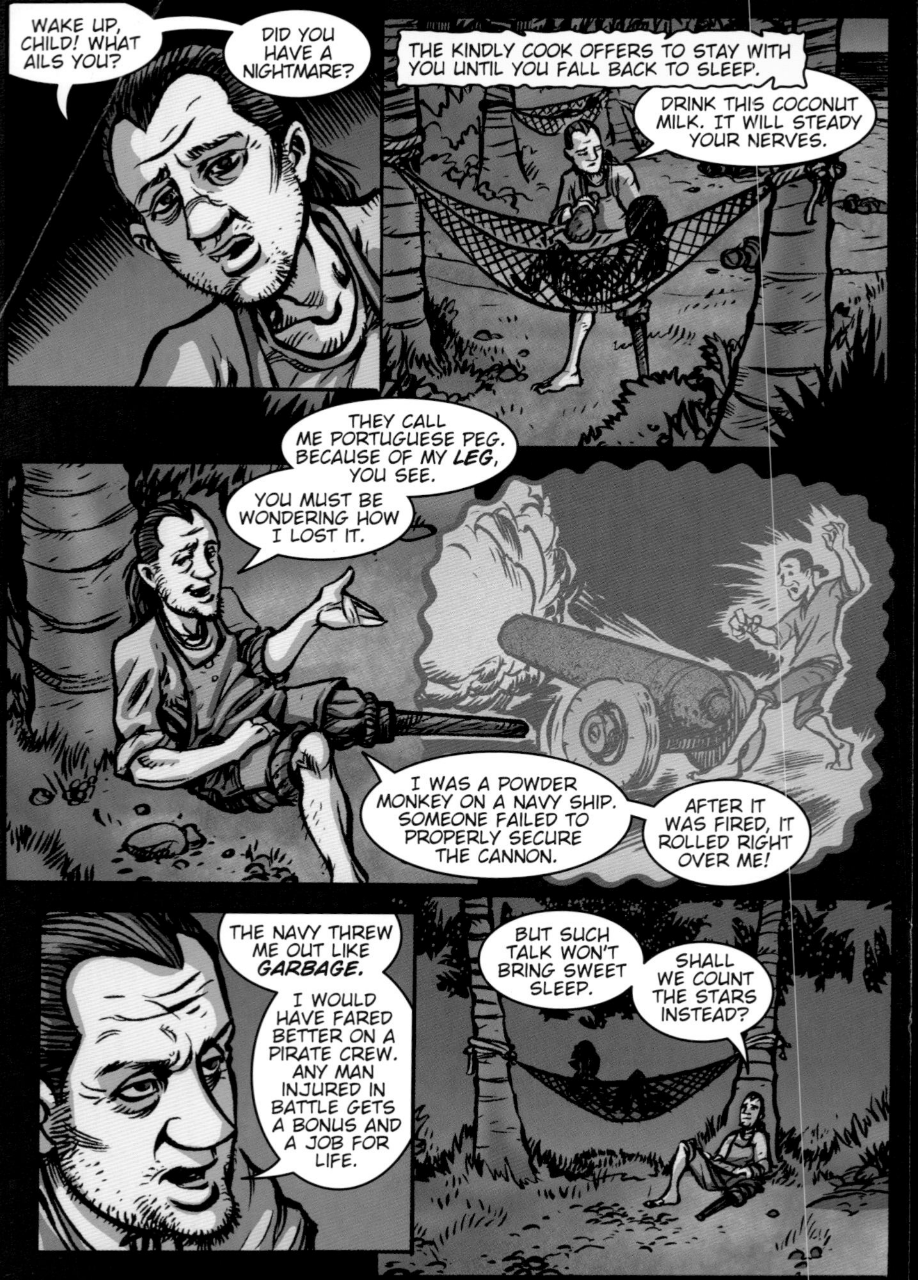
WAKE UP, CHILD! WHAT AILS YOU?
DID YOU HAVE A NIGHTMARE?
THE KINDLY COOK OFFERS TO STAY WITH YOU UNTIL YOU FALL BACK TO SLEEP.
DRINK THIS COCONUT MILK. IT WILL STEADY YOUR NERVES.
THEY CALL ME PORTUGUESE PEG. BECAUSE OF MY LEG, YOU SEE.
YOU MUST BE WONDERING HOW I LOST IT.
I WAS A POWDER MONKEY ON A NAVY SHIP. SOMEONE FAILED TO PROPERLY SECURE THE CANNON.
AFTER IT WAS FIRED, IT ROLLED RIGHT OVER ME!
THE NAVY THREW ME OUT LIKE GARBAGE.
I WOULD HAVE FARED BETTER ON A PIRATE CREW. ANY MAN INJURED IN BATTLE GETS A BONUS AND A JOB FOR LIFE.
BUT SUCH TALK WON'T BRING SWEET SLEEP.
SHALL WE COUNT THE STARS INSTEAD?

GO ON TO THE NEXT PAGE.

You wake early to a strange chattering sound. Your groggy eyes focus on a skinny, striped cat. The cat's tail swishes back and forth across the sand. Its back feet tense for the spring!

At first you don't know where you are. Then the terrible events of the previous day come rushing back. Higgins brought Stripes and her kittens from the *Endeavour*. And now the hungry momma cat is about to make breakfast out of the trumpet-playing pirate's parrot!

TURN TO PAGE 101.

When you join Father, Captain Jack wonders why the child of a rich man is as dirty as a common sailor. You explain about helping out in the pump room. Smoky Jack takes a liking to you. He offers to drop you at the next port—free of ransom.

You refuse to go without Father. Jack's men argue over whether to set you both free or "kill the stubborn brat."

While the buccaneers brawl, some of the loyal sailors free Captain Timothy and the officers. They grab weapons. A full-out fight follows. Shots fly among the buccaneers, mutineers, and men loyal to the *Endeavour*.

Father tries to pull you below decks. But you are struck by a stray bullet. Pain quickly yields to shock. As your body begins to shut down, you take comfort in the knowledge that you remained true to Father to the very last.

THE END

How will you try to escape? The pirates are less likely to find you in the jungle. But on the coast, you could find seafood to eat.

WILL YOU. . .

...venture into the jungle?

TURN TO PAGE 33.

...stay on the coast?

TURN TO PAGE 92.

The knife glances off the Spanish captain's elegant uniform. Your shout draws Jack's attention. But it also alerts a nearby Spanish sailor. He stabs you!

Captain Jack rushes to your side as your life's blood leaks onto the deck. The buccaneer swears, "I will find your father—and give him your share of the treasure." You scarcely have time to wonder if he's telling the truth. Your eyes close for the last time.

Captain Jack keeps his promise. Father uses his share of the treasure to return to London. There he writes a book about his adventures. His hope is to warn others away from the dangerous waters of the Caribbean. But instead, the tales of excitement and gold lure more bold young men to answer Fortune's call.

THE END

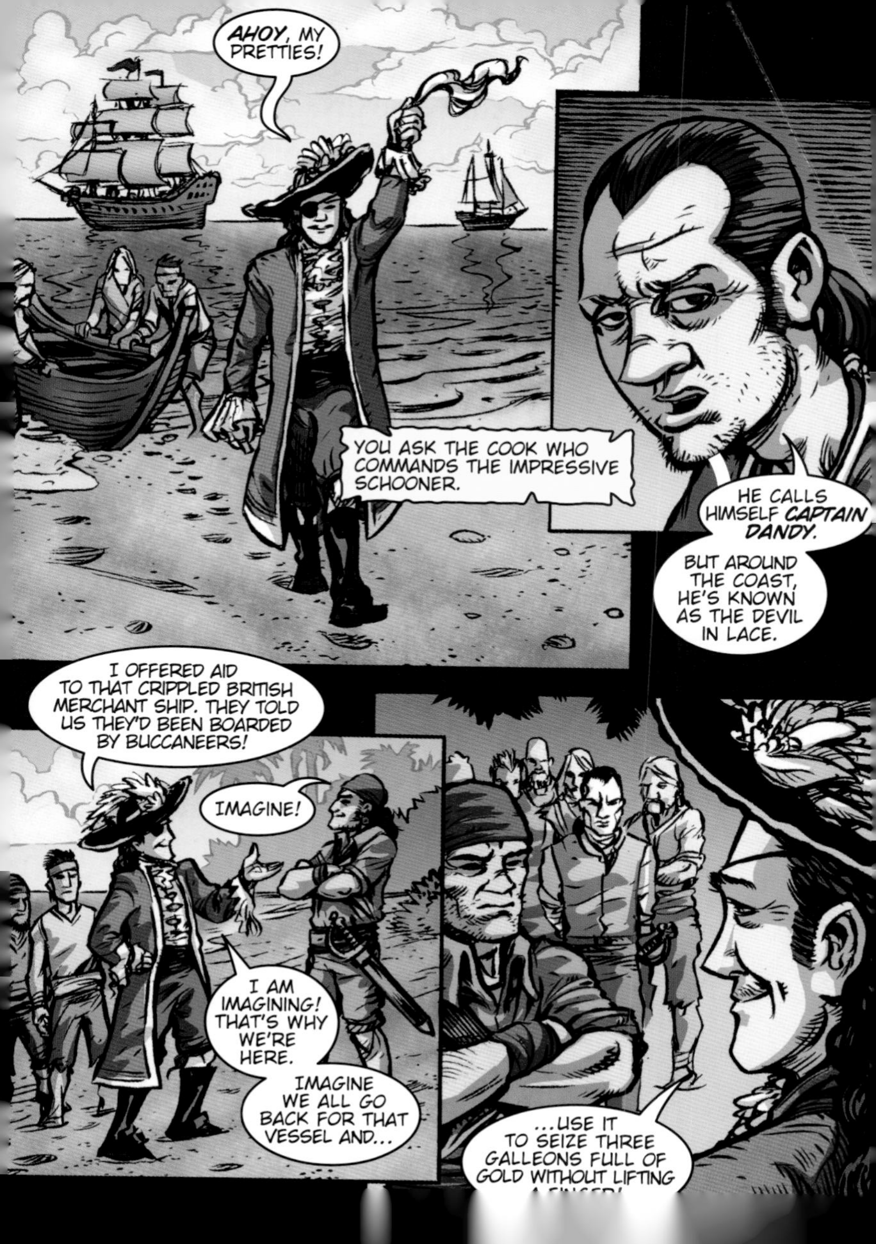
AHOY, MY PRETTIES!
YOU ASK THE COOK WHO COMMANDS THE IMPRESSIVE SCHOONER.
HE CALLS HIMSELF CAPTAIN DANDY.
BUT AROUND THE COAST, HE'S KNOWN AS THE DEVIL IN LACE.
I OFFERED AID TO THAT CRIPPLED BRITISH MERCHANT SHIP. THEY TOLD US THEY'D BEEN BOARDED BY BUCCANEERS!
IMAGINE!
I AM IMAGINING! THAT'S WHY WE'RE HERE.
IMAGINE WE ALL GO BACK FOR THAT VESSEL AND...
...USE IT TO SEIZE THREE GALLEONS FULL OF GOLD WITHOUT LIFTING

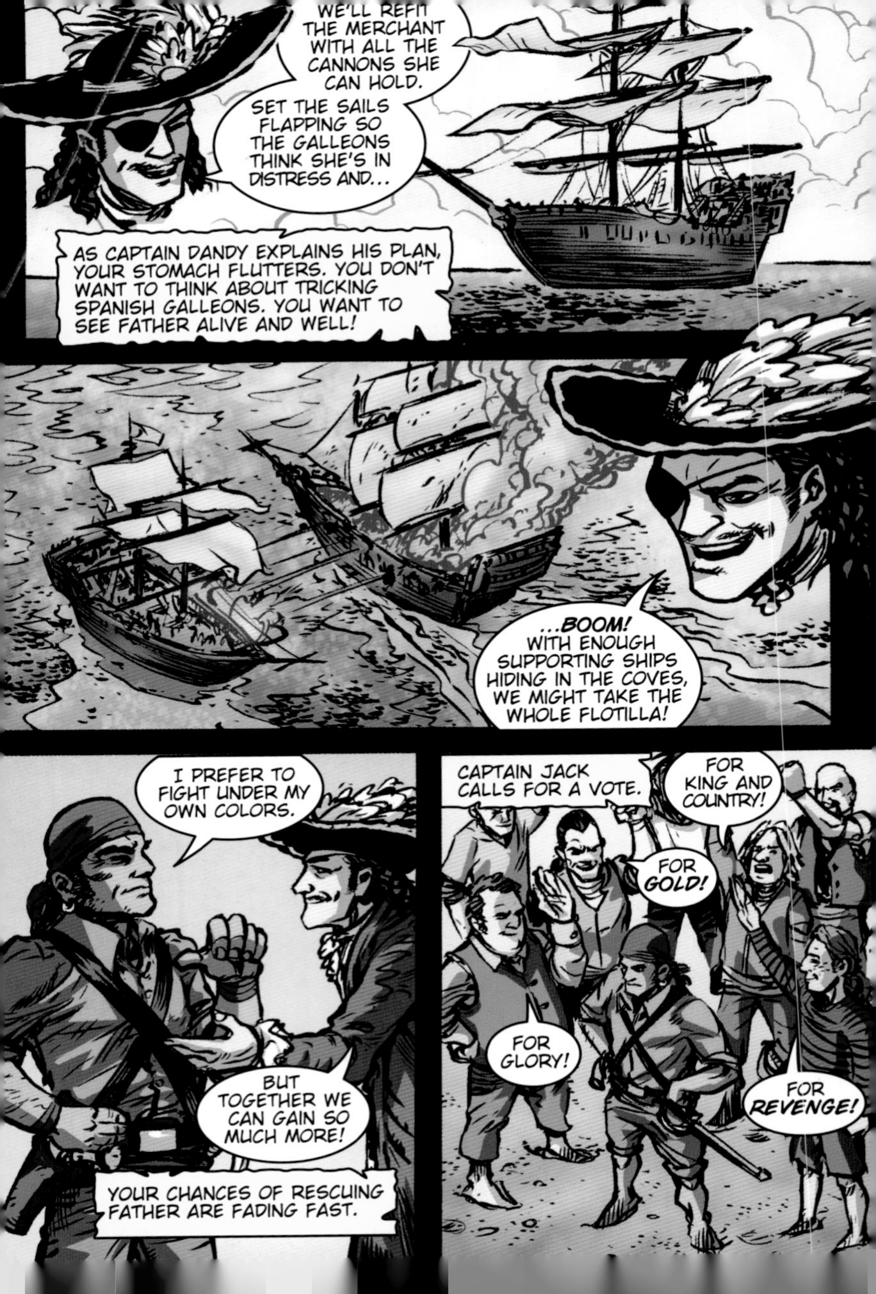

WE'LL REFIT THE MERCHANT WITH ALL THE CANNONS SHE CAN HOLD.
SET THE SAILS FLAPPING SO THE GALLEONS THINK SHE'S IN DISTRESS AND...
AS CAPTAIN DANDY EXPLAINS HIS PLAN, YOUR STOMACH FLUTTERS. YOU DON'T WANT TO THINK ABOUT TRICKING SPANISH GALLEONS. YOU WANT TO SEE FATHER ALIVE AND WELL!
...BOOM! WITH ENOUGH SUPPORTING SHIPS HIDING IN THE COVES, WE MIGHT TAKE THE WHOLE FLOTILLA!
I PREFER TO FIGHT UNDER MY OWN COLORS.
BUT TOGETHER WE CAN GAIN SO MUCH MORE!
YOUR CHANCES OF RESCUING FATHER ARE FADING FAST.
CAPTAIN JACK CALLS FOR A VOTE.
FOR KING AND COUNTRY!
FOR GOLD!
FOR GLORY!
FOR REVENGE!

"I'm sorry, child," Captain Jack says. "I know I promised we would return for your father this morning, but I am only a pirate captain. I cannot go against the will of my men."

"But Father's island isn't far from the *Endeavour*," you protest.

"You saw the vote," Jack replies.

You shudder, recalling the men's laughter when their captain reminded them of their promise. To the buccaneers, Father is just a joke, the Crab Master. But to you...

Captain Jack sees your expression. "Don't give up hope. After the raid, I'll rescue your fat old father, even if we have to go alone."

You want to believe him. But what good is a pirate's promise? And what if Captain Jack is killed during the raid? What will Father's chances be then?

You remember your promise to Captain Jack. You agreed not to try to escape or harm any of his crew. But what about Father?

WILL YOU...

...keep your promise in the hope that the pirate will keep his promise to you after the raid?

TURN TO PAGE 56.

...use your hidden knife to make sure Father is rescued right away?

TURN TO PAGE 109.

The dreaded articles contain many ideas you admire. They describe a way for free men to live together in respect. Profits are shared fairly, based on effort, skill, and risk.

Besides, your time with the buccaneers has given you an appetite not just for smoked meat, but for adventure. You sign your name and accept your share of the swag.

Captain Jack keeps his promise. Before long, you have found Father! He is much thinner but hasn't starved to death, thanks to the Arawak Indians. He has embraced their peaceful way of life—and even married an Arawak woman!

Father is glad for the "rescue." But he's disappointed when you tell him you have gone pirate. He wants nothing of you or your loot.

You are furious. After all you've done for him! You decide to stay with the pirates. You will forget you ever had another home.

THE END

WELCOME BACK!

LET'S SEE WHAT YOU CAUGHT!

THE PIRATE CAMP GETS READY FOR THE RAID. WHILE THE COOKS PREPARE THE SALAMAGUNDI, THE POWDER MONKEYS MAKE BULLETS.

YOU WANT TO HATE THE PIRATES FOR KEEPING YOU AWAY FROM FATHER. BUT YOU CANNOT HELP GETTING TO KNOW SOME OF THEM ALMOST AS FRIENDS.

GIVE US ANOTHER SONG, MUSICKER!

WHY DON'T WE CALL YOU *FIDDLES*?

CAN'T I GET A BETTER NAME THAN FRECKLES?

DO SOMETHING BOLD IN THE RAID AND YOU MIGHT EARN ONE!

YOU PLAY FOR THE PIRATES AS THE HOUR FOR THE RAID DRAWS NEAR.

EVEN THOUGH THE THOUGHT OF FIGHTING TERRIFIES YOU, YOU DECIDE THAT LATER YOU'LL HIDE THE KNIFE FROM YOUR VIOLIN CASE UNDER YOUR SHIRT. YOU ONLY HOPE YOU WON'T NEED TO USE IT.

Your body moves, but your mind is frozen with fear. You are on the sloop with Captain Jack and some of his crew, about to board the Spanish galleon.

Dandy and his men wait in the *Endeavour* for the Spanish galleon to approach. You think it's a rotten trick to pretend to need help and then blow up a ship, even a Spanish one. But you are hardly in a position to give orders. You just want to survive to rescue Father.

When the galleon comes in range, the *Endeavour* fires. BOOM! BOOM! BOOM!

Splinters rain from the smoky sky.

Captain Jack shouts, "Aboard!"

Pirates scramble all around you.

"Come, Fiddles! It's time we earned our keep," Gabby declares. He blows his trumpet. Drums bangs his drums, and you play the violin as loud as you can. But whistling shot and the screams of the wounded drown out the sound of the strings.

GO ON TO THE NEXT PAGE.

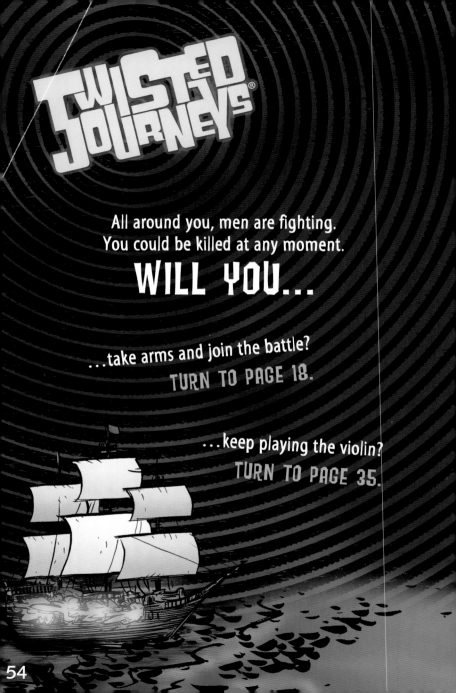

All around you, men are fighting.
You could be killed at any moment.

WILL YOU...

...take arms and join the battle?
TURN TO PAGE 18.

...keep playing the violin?
TURN TO PAGE 35.

You "bite the bullet" as the carpenter instructs. By the
time he burns the wound with a hot poker to stop the
bleeding, you have passed out.

You wake up, ranting with fever. After weeks of suffering, you pull through. By now poor Father must be dead.

With a hook on the end of your stump, you realize
you'll never be welcome in polite society again. You carve
out a life a reasonably happy life for yourself on the island
as a storyteller.

THE END

While many of the pirates go to retrieve the *Endeavour*, you're left in the hideout on Hispaniola. You hear Portuguese Peg and Sandy discussing recipes.

"It's called salamagundi," Peg raves. "And you won't find a finer dish on the seven seas. It takes a bit of everything: meat, fowl, fish, pickled vegetables, hard-boiled eggs, mangoes, cabbage, and olives. Simmer the whole mess in spiced wine. Then you season it with garlic, pepper, mustard seed, and just a splash of vinegar."

You've never heard of anything more disgusting! Sandy winks at you. Peg goes on. "Personally, I don't think salamagundi is complete without fresh crab meat."

"I could show you some good crab cakes," Sandy says.

Eager for something to do, you volunteer to catch some crabs for the cooks.

56   TURN TO PAGE 93.

WILL YOU...

...save as much food as you can to share with the men below decks?

TURN TO PAGE 11.

...protect the sailors' feelings by never mentioning the treats you enjoy at the captain's table?

TURN TO PAGE 28.

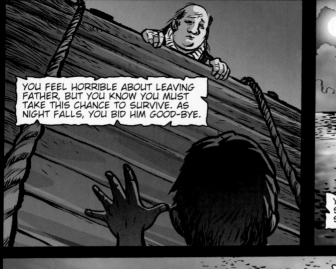

YOU FEEL HORRIBLE ABOUT LEAVING FATHER, BUT YOU KNOW YOU MUST TAKE THIS CHANCE TO SURVIVE. AS NIGHT FALLS, YOU BID HIM GOOD-BYE.

YOU WONDER IF THE SHIP WILL EVER SIGHT LAND OR...

...IF YOU WILL BE LOST AT SEA.

LAND!

UNFORTUNATELY, THE LAND IS OCCUPIED BY CANNIBALS. THEY ARE HUNGRY, AND WHILE YOU'RE NOT AS TASTY AS A FRENCHMAN, YOU'LL DO!

THE END

You pounce on the cat just before Stripes can pounce on the parrot. As the bird flutters up off the sand, you hold the cat gently in your arms.

You put Stripes down near Higgins and the kittens. As soon as the mother cat lies down, the kittens begin to nurse. Their gentle purring joins the chorus of snores in the sleepy pirate camp.

You realize this is an opportunity. You look around. The buccaneers are surrounded by knives, cutlasses, pistols, blunderbusses, and other weapons. But what can you grab without waking anyone?

You spot a knife sticking out of the sand. It's fallen from a pirate's belt as he sleeps. You seize the weapon, hoping you won't need it. You hide it in your violin case.

GO ON TO THE NEXT PAGE

When Gabby finds out you rescued Rosy, he offers the bird to you.

"I'm tired of her chewing my ear and relieving herself on my shoulder," the pirate explains. "And if that isn't bad enough, she squawks every time someone sneezes."

While the buccaneers eat breakfast, you get to know your new pet. Rosy keeps you from being too restless about rescuing Father.

You share your food with the bright bird. "God save the King!" you say.

Rosy blinks.

"God save the King!" you repeat.

And to your amazement, the parrot parrots back, "God save the King!"

You sneeze.

Rosy ducks her head and squawks. "God save the King!"

You sneeze again, and Rosy repeats her lesson. You can't wait to show your new prize to Father. But just as you and the pirates are about to set off for the island...

TURN TO PAGE 47.

WILL YOU...

...make the leap? A bold move could mean the difference between life and death.

TURN TO PAGE 62.

...keep your word? Maybe honor means more to you than freedom. Besides, a better chance of escape might present itself in the pirate camp.

TURN TO PAGE 94.

You swim as far as you can, hoping by some miracle to find land. The tropical sun beats down on your head without mercy. You're so tired, you're tempted to give up.

Then you hear a bird shriek. Land must be near! Yes, you can just make it out on the horizon. You kick with renewed strength. Each stroke of your exhausted arms pulls you closer to your goal.

Then something tugs at one of your legs. You feel surrounded by sudden warmth, and you sense something large beneath you.

You look down and wonder why the turquoise sea has turned such a bright red. Then you realize the dark presence is a SHARK!

Mighty jaws pull you under the red-tinged waters. Before the pain can begin, you pass out.

THE END

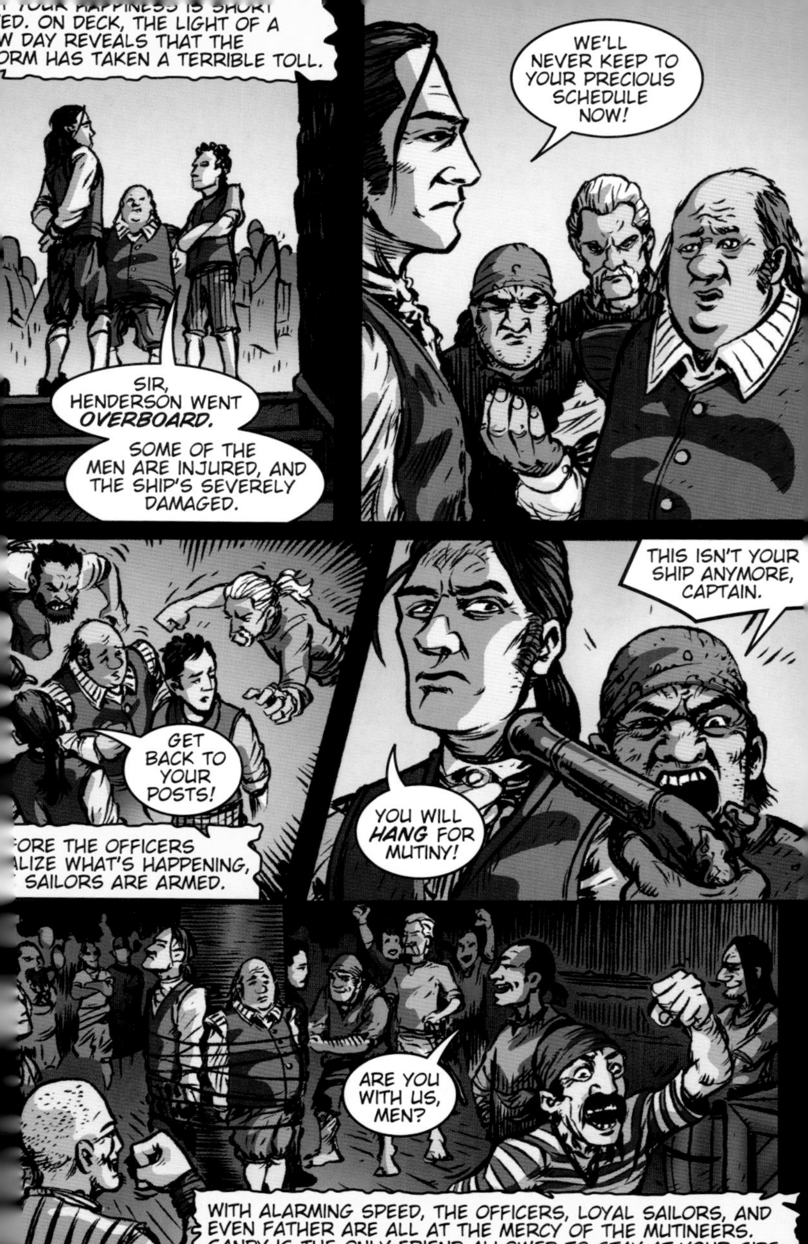
ED. ON DECK, THE LIGHT OF A W DAY REVEALS THAT THE ORM HAS TAKEN A TERRIBLE TOLL.
WE'LL NEVER KEEP TO YOUR PRECIOUS SCHEDULE NOW!
SIR, HENDERSON WENT OVERBOARD.
SOME OF THE MEN ARE INJURED, AND THE SHIP'S SEVERELY DAMAGED.
GET BACK TO YOUR POSTS!
ORE THE OFFICERS ALIZE WHAT'S HAPPENING, SAILORS ARE ARMED.
THIS ISN'T YOUR SHIP ANYMORE, CAPTAIN.
YOU WILL HANG FOR MUTINY!
ARE YOU WITH US, MEN?
WITH ALARMING SPEED, THE OFFICERS, LOYAL SAILORS, AND EVEN FATHER ARE ALL AT THE MERCY OF THE MUTINEERS. SANDY IS THE ONLY FRIEND ALLOWED TO STAY AT YOUR SIDE.

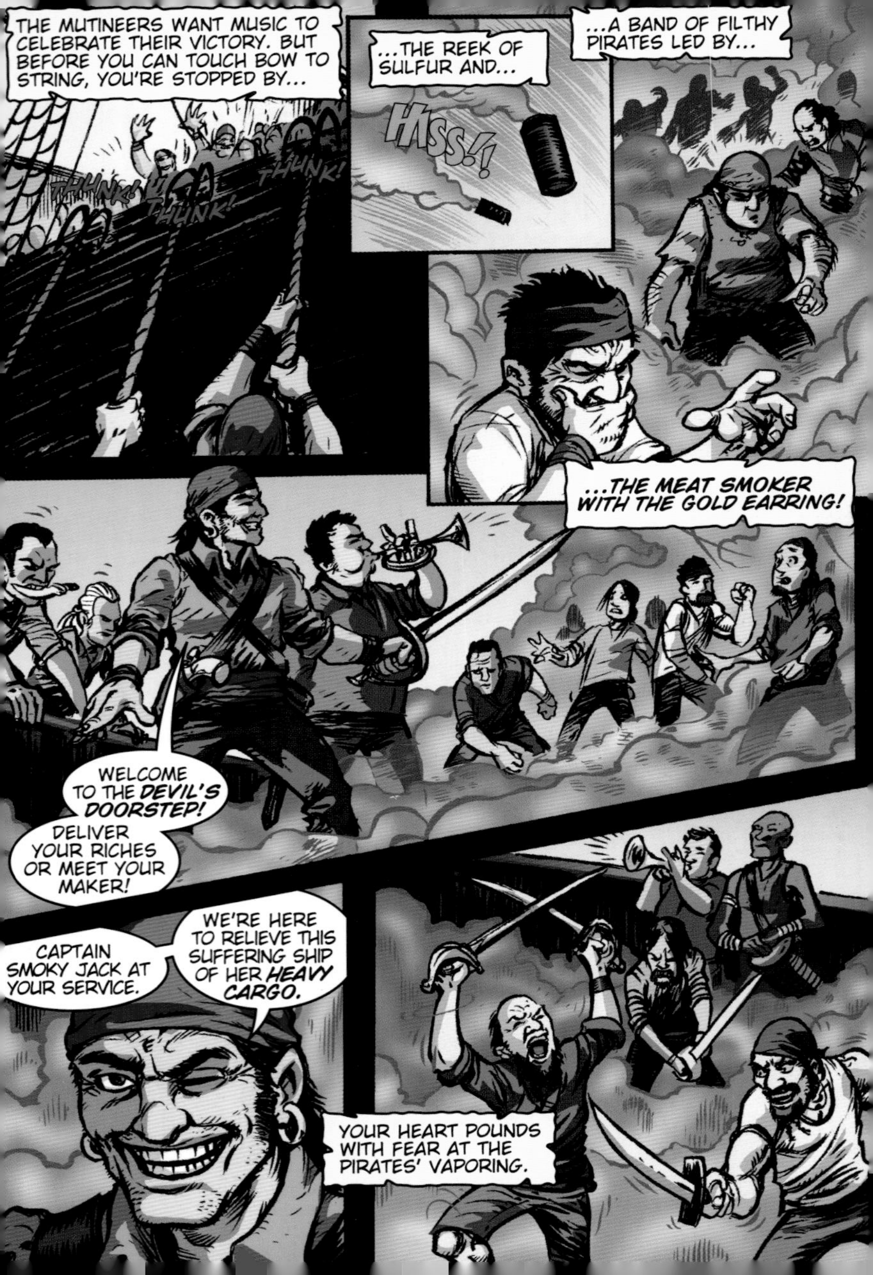
THE MUTINEERS WANT MUSIC TO CELEBRATE THEIR VICTORY. BUT BEFORE YOU CAN TOUCH BOW TO STRING, YOU'RE STOPPED BY...
THUNK!
THUNK!
THUNK!
...THE REEK OF SULFUR AND...
HISS!!
...A BAND OF FILTHY PIRATES LED BY...
...THE MEAT SMOKER WITH THE GOLD EARRING!
WELCOME TO THE DEVIL'S DOORSTEP!
DELIVER YOUR RICHES OR MEET YOUR MAKER!
CAPTAIN SMOKY JACK AT YOUR SERVICE.
WE'RE HERE TO RELIEVE THIS SUFFERING SHIP OF HER HEAVY CARGO.
YOUR HEART POUNDS WITH FEAR AT THE PIRATES' VAPORING.

Smoky Jack looks hard at Captain Timothy. "Will you surrender your cargo— or die for some rich man's profit?"

The captain stares back. "It appears we are in no position to bargain."

The pirate laughs and then bows to the mutineers. "Thank you for wrapping things up so neatly."

Templeton bristles. "Why should we give up our loot to you?"

In a flash, Smoky Jack crosses the deck to land beside Templeton. Even faster, Jack's shiny cutlass is at the sailor's skinny throat. "If you prefer, you may leave it to me in your will."

Templeton's eyes widen. "No need for violence."

Captain Jack smiles. "Brothers, why not sign the articles and join us?"

"What does he mean?" you whisper to Sandy.

"Articles are an agreement pirates sign when they join a crew," the cook replies.

GO ON TO THE NEXT PAGE.

Suddenly, Smoky Jack's eyes are right on you! But your face is still filthy from your work in the pump room. You look like a common sailor.

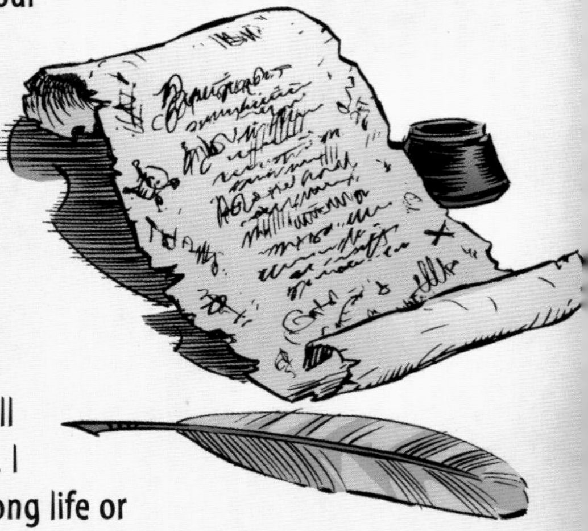

Smoky Jack tells the crew, "The articles guarantee that each man gets his fair share of the loot—a better deal than any of you will see on this sinking ship. I cannot promise you a long life or an easy one, but you will have treasure, pleasure, and a chance to make the Spaniards weep!"

"What will you do with us?" Captain Timothy demands.

"That is up to you," the buccaneer leader answers. "Those capable of honest toil on the seas may sign the articles and share the swag."

"And if we refuse?" Captain Timothy asks.

"Stay on your sinking ship." Then he turns to the passengers. "Any of you who prefer being ransomed to staying with the ship are also welcome to join us."

TURN TO PAGE 88.

What if Higgins is stealing more than just cream? If he takes too many supplies, his crime could put the safety of the ship at stake.

WILL YOU...

...decide not to tell yet, but follow Higgins to see where he goes with the cream?

TURN TO PAGE 98.

...tell Father about the incident, trusting that he and the captain will know the best thing to do?

TURN TO PAGE 107.

You spend four terrifying days at sea. Then the long-boat lands on a tiny island.

You're relieved to discover that the only people here are members of the Arawak tribe. These kindly people have no word for war.

Some of the mutineers stay to live peacefully on the island. Others leave to join various pirate bands in the area.

You stay with the Arawaks. They teach you their special way of smoking meat. You learn to butcher cows. You become a skillful hunter. You spend many pleasant days stalking wild pigs and other tasty prey.

When you grow older, you marry and raise a family. You're happy enough. But you're always haunted by the thought that you left Father to an unknown fate.

THE END

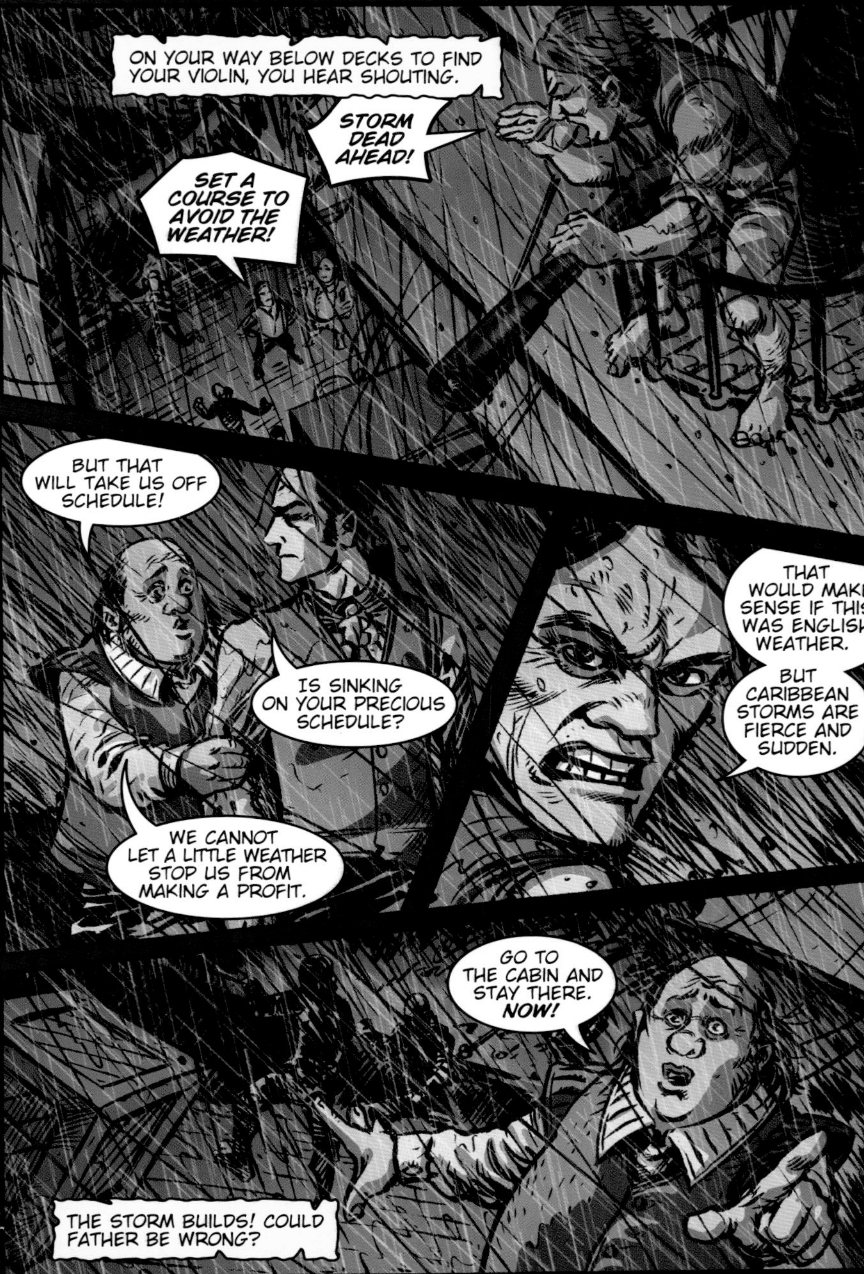
ON YOUR WAY BELOW DECKS TO FIND YOUR VIOLIN, YOU HEAR SHOUTING.
STORM DEAD AHEAD!
SET A COURSE TO AVOID THE WEATHER!
BUT THAT WILL TAKE US OFF SCHEDULE!
IS SINKING ON YOUR PRECIOUS SCHEDULE?
WE CANNOT LET A LITTLE WEATHER STOP US FROM MAKING A PROFIT.
THAT WOULD MAKE SENSE IF THIS WAS ENGLISH WEATHER.
BUT CARIBBEAN STORMS ARE FIERCE AND SUDDEN.
GO TO THE CABIN AND STAY THERE. NOW!
THE STORM BUILDS! COULD FATHER BE WRONG?

GO ON TO THE NEXT PAGE.

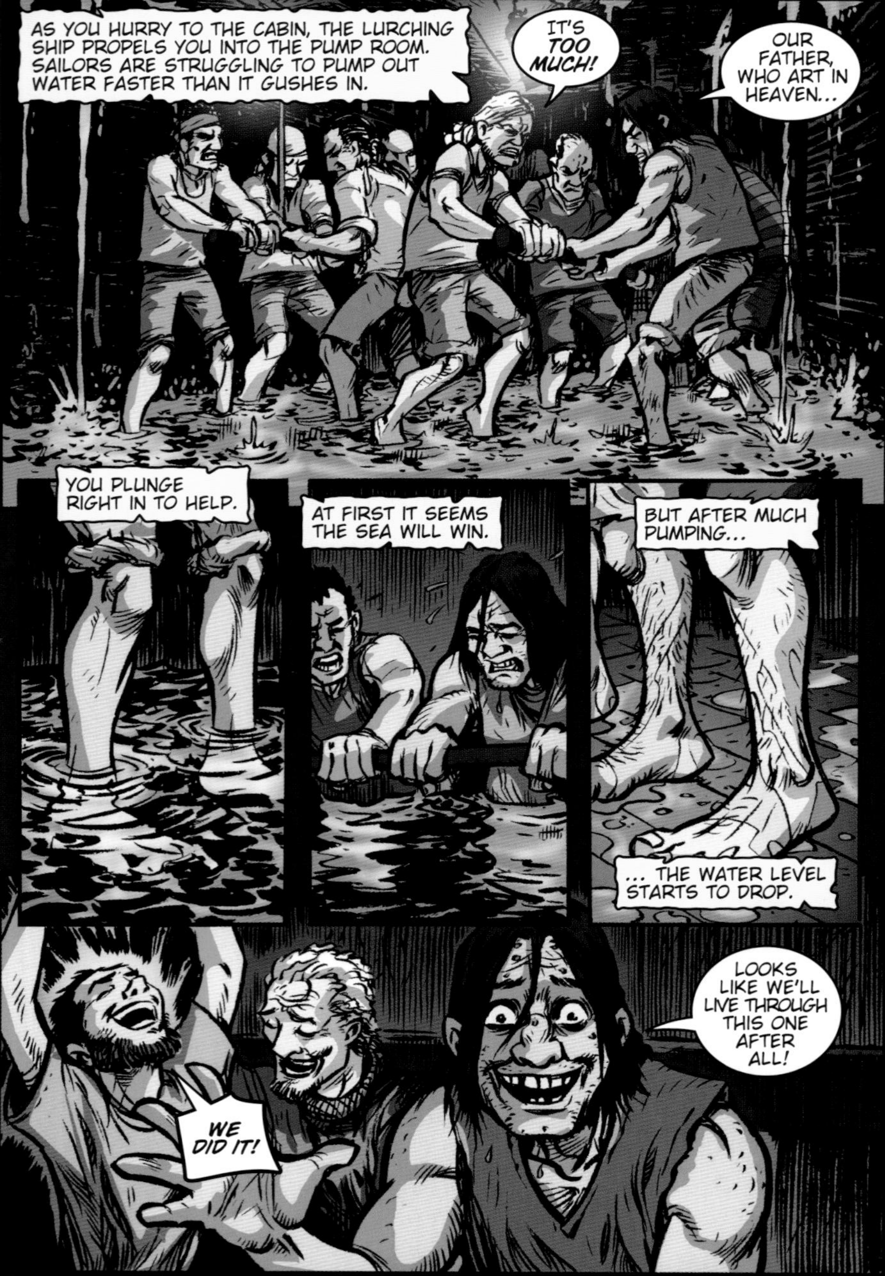
AS YOU HURRY TO THE CABIN, THE LURCHING SHIP PROPELS YOU INTO THE PUMP ROOM. SAILORS ARE STRUGGLING TO PUMP OUT WATER FASTER THAN IT GUSHES IN.
IT'S TOO MUCH!
OUR FATHER, WHO ART IN HEAVEN...
YOU PLUNGE RIGHT IN TO HELP.
AT FIRST IT SEEMS THE SEA WILL WIN.
BUT AFTER MUCH PUMPING...
... THE WATER LEVEL STARTS TO DROP.
LOOKS LIKE WE'LL LIVE THROUGH THIS ONE AFTER ALL!
WE DID IT!

TURN TO PAGE 63.

Even as you sign the articles, you feel a black bitterness enter your heart. The history lessons Father forced you to learn turn out to be useful. You remember many battle plans from long-ago wars. This knowledge helps you lead successful raids, and you quickly rise in the ranks. Finally, you split off to lead your own pirate gang.

Your upper-class background also comes in handy. You become known for your elegant ways. You dine with plantation owners and government officials. Soon you rule your own island.

Then the English government cracks down on pirates. You become rich by betraying your former friends. You die wealthy on a plantation full of slaves. You are buried in a silk-lined coffin. But just months after your death, a storm ravages the island and the sea swallows your grave.

THE END

WILL YOU. . .

. . .let the carpenter cut off your hand?
TURN TO PAGE 55.

. . .tough it out with a bandage?
TURN TO PAGE 108.

"If you prove a good musicker, we'll come back for your fat father soon," Captain Jack says. "Promise on your honor not to try to escape or to harm any of us."

You agree. You struggle to keep a stiff upper lip as strong pirates lower Father into a longboat.

"Three cheers for the Crab Master!" someone shouts. And all the pirates cheer.

Your eyes are locked on Father's. He nods, and you know he wants you to be brave. You press your lips together and nod back.

You watch as the small boat becomes even smaller on the vast sea. You wonder if you should have gone with Father. But you tell yourself you have a better chance of helping him by staying with the pirates than by starving at his side. You hope you're right!

GO ON TO THE NEXT PAGE.

Pirates surround you as you climb down from the *Endeavour* onto Captain Jack's sloop. SNAP! The rain-freshened breeze fills the sloop's single large sail.

The narrow ship is so fast, it seems to fly over the turquoise water. Under other circumstances, this would be heavenly. But your stomach is knotted with fear—not just for yourself but for Father.

You are an excellent swimmer. You wonder if you should just dive into the water before anyone can stop you. It would mean breaking your promise and probably drowning, but that might be better than the fate that awaits you in the pirates' hideout.

TURN TO PAGE 61.

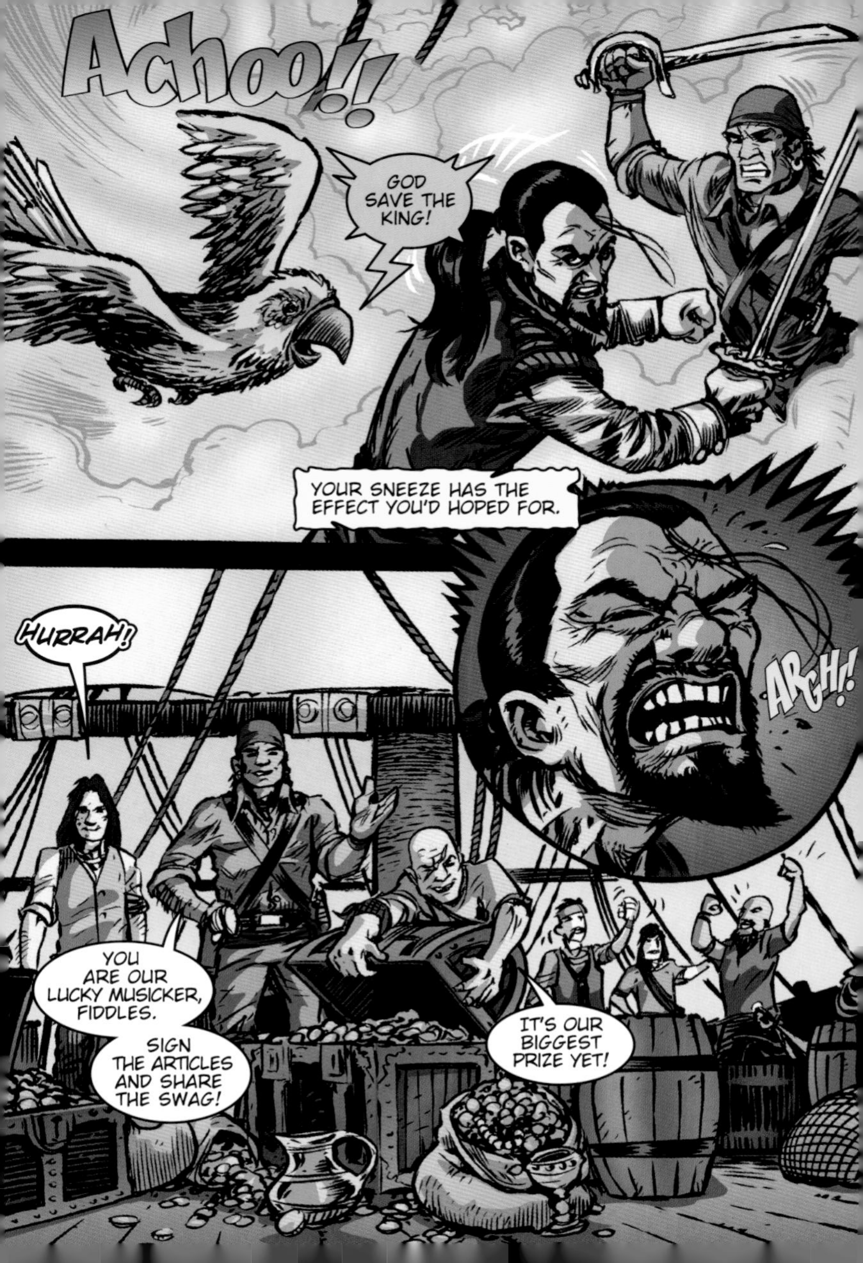
Achoo!!
GOD SAVE THE KING!
YOUR SNEEZE HAS THE EFFECT YOU'D HOPED FOR.
ARGH!!
HURRAH!
YOU ARE OUR LUCKY MUSICKER, FIDDLES.
SIGN THE ARTICLES AND SHARE THE SWAG!
IT'S OUR BIGGEST PRIZE YET!

As you read the articles, you're surprised. They describe a fair way of life, based on sharing and skill. But still—it's a life of crime!

WILL YOU. . .

. . .sign the articles?
TURN TO PAGE 51.

. . .once again refuse to declare yourself a pirate?
TURN TO PAGE 38.

After several weeks, the *Endeavour* arrives in the Caribbean. Eager to stay on schedule, Father forces the captain to keep a straight course through a storm. The ship almost goes under.

When the skies clear, angry sailors seize the ship! The mutineers plan to repair the *Endeavour* and sail her under a pirate flag.

"You will hang for this!" Father threatens.

"Not before you drown!" laughs Squid.

The mutineers force the other sailors to choose between joining them or walking the plank with the officers.

"What about the passengers?" Templeton wonders.

"We'll put them to port— for a price," Squid replies.

"Even the fat fool who nearly sank the ship?" Templeton asks.

"Shoot him!" someone shouts.

You gasp, realizing they mean Father!

"And what about the brat?" Templeton says. "Now that the ship is ours, perhaps the child won't be too good to play the fiddle for us."

TURN TO PAGE 84.

Captain Dandy tries for larger and larger scores to please his greedy crew. One day he takes on a well-armed galleon. The sea hunters find themselves captured.

You are thrown into a Spanish prison for trial. Here you learn of the "ultimate punishment." Some buccaneers are hung by the neck, then left to rot in a gibbet. You shudder at the thought of your corpse caged in metal and strung up in the harbor as an example to would-be pirates.

Dandy's crew reminds you that you never signed the articles. You are young and have never committed a crime. You may yet be released.

GO ON TO THE NEXT PAGE.

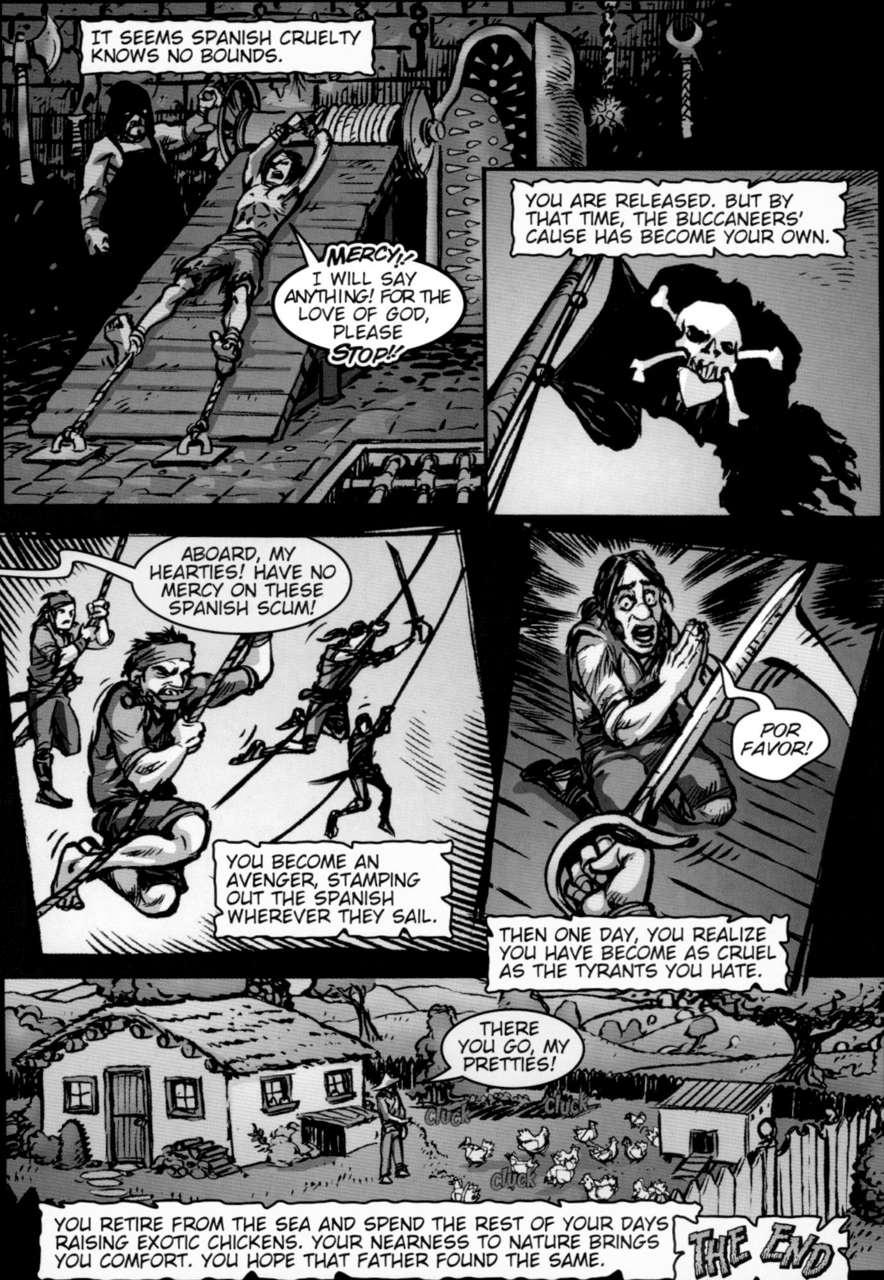

IT SEEMS SPANISH CRUELTY KNOWS NO BOUNDS.
MERCY!! I WILL SAY ANYTHING! FOR THE LOVE OF GOD, PLEASE STOP!!
YOU ARE RELEASED. BUT BY THAT TIME, THE BUCCANEERS' CAUSE HAS BECOME YOUR OWN.
ABOARD, MY HEARTIES! HAVE NO MERCY ON THESE SPANISH SCUM!
YOU BECOME AN AVENGER, STAMPING OUT THE SPANISH WHEREVER THEY SAIL.
POR FAVOR!
THEN ONE DAY, YOU REALIZE YOU HAVE BECOME AS CRUEL AS THE TYRANTS YOU HATE.
THERE YOU GO, MY PRETTIES!
cluck
cluck
cluck
YOU RETIRE FROM THE SEA AND SPEND THE REST OF YOUR DAYS RAISING EXOTIC CHICKENS. YOUR NEARNESS TO NATURE BRINGS YOU COMFORT. YOU HOPE THAT FATHER FOUND THE SAME.
THE END

As you and Father climb from the longboat, he hands you the pistol and bullets. You quickly load the weapon.

WILL YOU. . .

. . .save the bullets in the hope of finding some wild game?

TURN TO PAGE 110.

. . .shoot the pirate?

TURN TO PAGE 111.

You sprint as fast as you can through the trees. Behind you, you hear growls. The beasts are wild dogs—and they're catching up!

In your panic, you trip and fall down a hill. The dogs decide not to pursue you down the dangerous slope.

You're not sure what's broken or just bruised. You try to sit up, but dizziness knocks you down.

Rosy squawks. "God save the King!" The parrot pecks at you playfully, hoping for food. "God save the King!"

As your eyes shut, perhaps for the last time, you see the hungry bird fly away.

You awaken under the gaze of a friendly Arawak man. He points to Rosy, who holds a piece of meat in her beak. You realize your pet must have followed the smell of roasting meat to an Arawak camp.

GO ON TO THE NEXT PAGE.

The Arawaks carry you to their camp to tend your wounds. Over many months, you learn their ways and come to love them. But you never forget Father. The tribe helps you search for him.

You have no luck finding Father. But one day, you are found. A hunting party from an English navy ship returns you to "civilization." By now, you've spent too much time leading the natural life of the Arawaks to go home happily. English society is no longer your cup of tea.

You always wonder what happened to Father. You like to think that he also was adopted by Arawaks and managed to find some happiness.

THE END

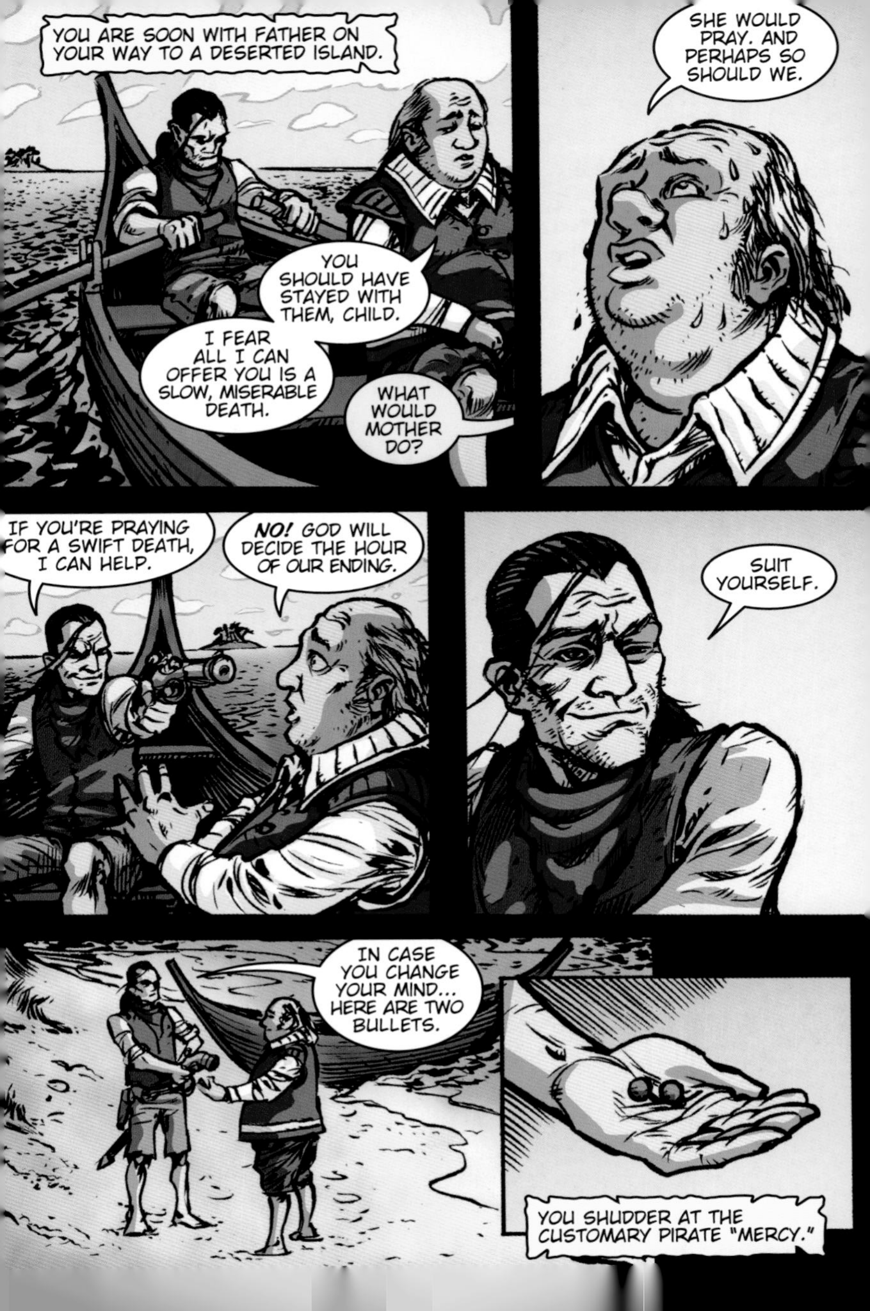
YOU ARE SOON WITH FATHER ON YOUR WAY TO A DESERTED ISLAND.
YOU SHOULD HAVE STAYED WITH THEM, CHILD.
I FEAR ALL I CAN OFFER YOU IS A SLOW, MISERABLE DEATH.
WHAT WOULD MOTHER DO?
SHE WOULD PRAY. AND PERHAPS SO SHOULD WE.
IF YOU'RE PRAYING FOR A SWIFT DEATH, I CAN HELP.
NO! GOD WILL DECIDE THE HOUR OF OUR ENDING.
SUIT YOURSELF.
IN CASE YOU CHANGE YOUR MIND... HERE ARE TWO BULLETS.
YOU SHUDDER AT THE CUSTOMARY PIRATE "MERCY."

WILL YOU. . .

...refuse to cooperate, even though it may mean walking the plank?

TURN TO PAGE 89.

...pretend to agree to play a song, then try to escape?

TURN TO PAGE 102.

Working in stolen moments, you hide materials in the lowest hold. Slowly you build a raft out of spare planks and rope. Empty wine casks will help the raft float.

One night, Dandy's men are snoring after celebrating a big score. You slip the raft into the ocean without being seen. By a miracle of good fortune, you reach a deserted island.

You are not bothered by pirates or cannibals. But loneliness drives you mad. You become especially upset when you think of Father. Did he suffer a fate like your own? Did he even survive?

THE END

You're surprised at how many sailors play music, sing, and dance.

"We'd go mad without music!" Rusty exclaims.

"Even pirates have music," remarks an old salt named Smitty. "It's part of their vaporing."

"What's vaporing?" you wonder.

"It's a way pirates have of scaring their prey. They clang their cutlasses together and dance like wild beasts. And they shout threats," Smitty explains. "They like to have music while they vapor—and while they eat and make merry."

"I've heard pirate musickers get a bigger share than regular crew," says a skinny sailor named Templeton.

"At least they all get a share!" grumbles Squid, his short companion.

All eyes flick to you nervously. Unlike pirates, these men won't share in the profits from this voyage. You know they don't get paid much. But you suppose these sailors should be glad for honest work with Father's company.

GO ON TO THE NEXT PAGE.

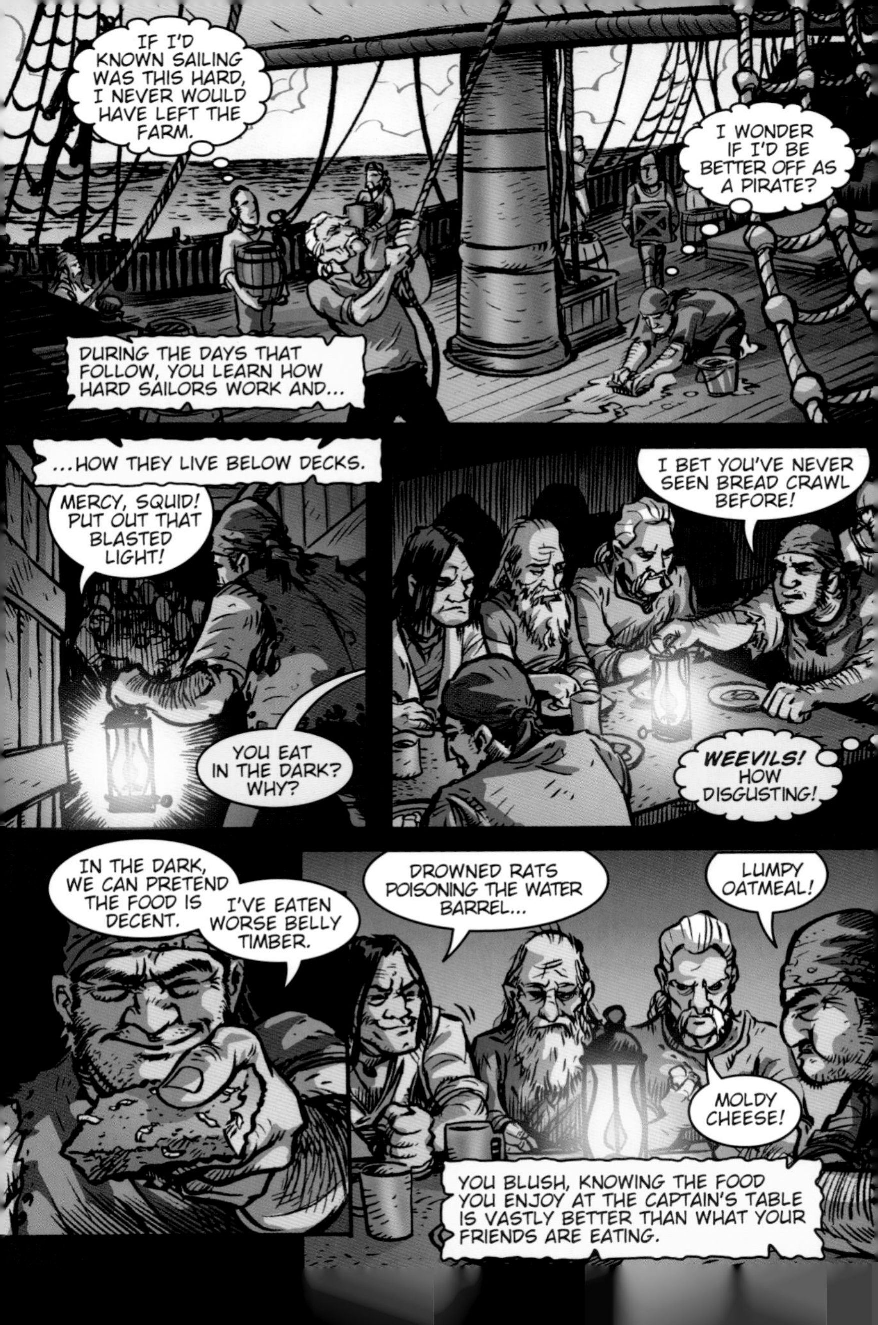
IF I'D KNOWN SAILING WAS THIS HARD, I NEVER WOULD HAVE LEFT THE FARM.
I WONDER IF I'D BE BETTER OFF AS A PIRATE?
DURING THE DAYS THAT FOLLOW, YOU LEARN HOW HARD SAILORS WORK AND...
...HOW THEY LIVE BELOW DECKS.
MERCY, SQUID! PUT OUT THAT BLASTED LIGHT!
YOU EAT IN THE DARK? WHY?
I BET YOU'VE NEVER SEEN BREAD CRAWL BEFORE!
WEEVILS! HOW DISGUSTING!
IN THE DARK, WE CAN PRETEND THE FOOD IS DECENT.
I'VE EATEN WORSE BELLY TIMBER.
DROWNED RATS POISONING THE WATER BARREL...
LUMPY OATMEAL!
MOLDY CHEESE!
YOU BLUSH, KNOWING THE FOOD YOU ENJOY AT THE CAPTAIN'S TABLE IS VASTLY BETTER THAN WHAT YOUR FRIENDS ARE EATING.

There's no telling what the buccaneers will do if they discover your true identity. But you can't imagine abandoning Father.

WILL YOU. . .

...keep quiet for the moment?

TURN TO PAGE 10.

...step forward to join Father and the other passengers?

TURN TO PAGE 44.

"At least free my hands so I can swim," you beg, just before the mutineers toss you into the salty sea.

They laugh cruelly as they comply. "Enjoy your exercise!"

You know they're laughing because the nearest land is much too far to reach by swimming. But you're determined to try. Perhaps if you swim fast enough, you won't have to hear them shoot Father.

You swim until your arms feel like lead, then turn over and float on your back. You look up at the sky, so beautifully fresh now that the storm has passed. You see a rainbow and wonder if it will be the last sight you enjoy in this lifetime.

GO ON TO THE NEXT PAGE.

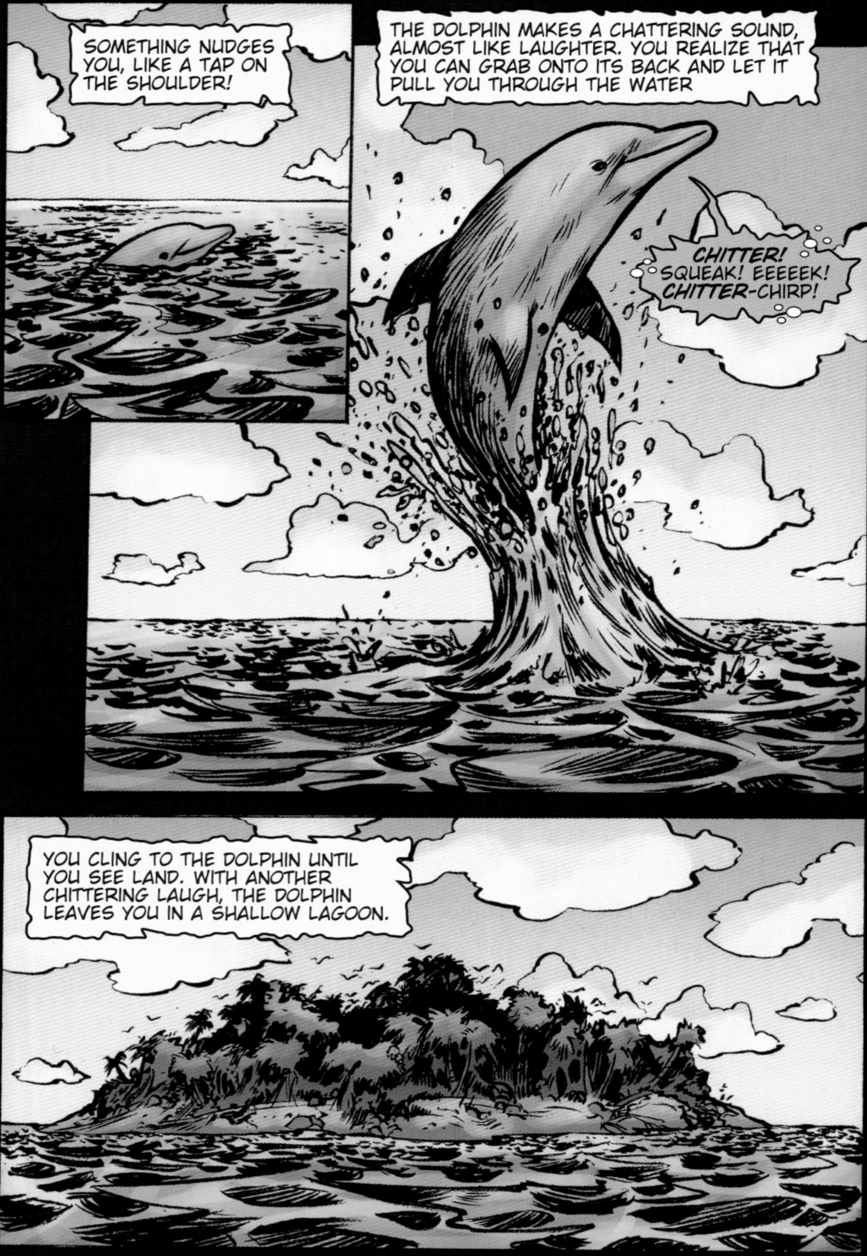
SOMETHING NUDGES YOU, LIKE A TAP ON THE SHOULDER!
THE DOLPHIN MAKES A CHATTERING SOUND, ALMOST LIKE LAUGHTER. YOU REALIZE THAT YOU CAN GRAB ONTO ITS BACK AND LET IT PULL YOU THROUGH THE WATER
CHITTER! SQUEAK! EEEEEK! CHITTER-CHIRP!
YOU CLING TO THE DOLPHIN UNTIL YOU SEE LAND. WITH ANOTHER CHITTERING LAUGH, THE DOLPHIN LEAVES YOU IN A SHALLOW LAGOON.

GO ON TO THE NEXT PAGE.

The island is uninhabited, except for tasty crabs and other wildlife. At first you fear loneliness will drive you mad. But your struggle to survive puts you in touch with the island's animals.

You make friends with parrots, monkeys, and even wild pigs. You learn to use the materials around you to make tools, like a fishing pole and hooks. You build a simple shelter and a pen for raising pigs.

You miss Father and the many comforts of home. But you discover a kind of peace in this natural life. Many years later, stories of survivors like you inspire Daniel Defoe to write his classic book *Robinson Crusoe*.

THE END

The pirates follow your footprints in the sand. You run as fast as you can but are soon recaptured by the angry crew. You have broken your promise! Following a brief trial, you are marooned on an island.

Before you can starve, your luck grows worse. A bite from an infected mosquito gives you malaria. In the fever dreams that follow, you go to a happy place where Mother is still alive. You play the violin for her on a gently drifting rowboat.

You die without ever realizing that this is only a dream.

THE END

You know that this isn't just a chance to stay busy. It's also an opportunity to escape from the buccaneers.

WILL YOU...

...sneak off on your own?

TURN TO PAGE 45.

...get the crabs and return to the pirate camp as you promised?

TURN TO PAGE 52.

After several tense hours at sea, a low island appears. Captain Jack's sloop speeds toward a lonely cove on Hispaniola. You try to remember everything you see. Maybe someday you'll be able to testify against these criminals. If you're ever rescued, that is.

Working quickly together, the pirates unload the *Endeavour*'s cargo. The sight reminds you of Father. You wonder where he is right now. Will he ever look up from his morning tea to smile at you again? You want to cry but refuse to let yourself.

GO ON TO THE NEXT PAGE.

WHILE THE QUARTERMASTER SORTS THE PRIZE INTO EQUAL SHARES, THE PIRATES CELEBRATE THEIR EASY VICTORY.

NOT A SHOT FIRED NOR A MAN HURT.

AND LOOK AT THOSE *GOOD* THEY'LL FETCH PRETTY PRICE.

TRY TO EAT SOMETHING.

YOU WERE KIND TO US ON THE *ENDEAVOUR*.

WE'LL DO WHAT WE CAN FOR YOU AND YOUR FATHER.

THIS IS THE BEST WE COULD GET.

YOU ARE MORE FRIGHTENED, TIRED, AND HUNGRY THAN YOU'VE EVER BEEN. THE SMELL OF ROASTING MEAT MAKES YOUR STOMACH GROWL.

GO ON TO THE NEXT PAGE

Your stomach turns. The strange stew of mystery meat has chunks of everything from boiled eggs to pickles. But you know that as a prisoner you can't be choosy.

WILL YOU...

...eat what you've been given?
TURN TO PAGE 34.

...turn up your nose and tighten your belt?
TURN TO PAGE 39.

Someone cries, "Help!" You look down from the rigging and see Rickets fall overboard! You grab a rope and swing down. From the deck, you hope to throw the powder monkey a line.

But when you land on the deck, a Spanish sailor blocks your path. You pull the knife from your belt and fight your way free. But your own momentum tumbles you overboard!

Cold water shocks your eyes wide open. The sea is red with blood from dead and dying men. Rickets disappears below the churning waters. You see a shark fin and real-ize that neither one of you will survive.

All you can do now is to call your angel in heaven. "Mother!"

THE END

Higgins hurries down to the darkest part of the lowest hold. You wonder if he heard you follow. Is he leading you into a trap? Or feeding a dangerous stowaway?

You're tempted to turn around, to run as fast as you can! Then you hear the distinctive squeak of kittens. Higgins's gruff voice croons gently, "Who's a hungry momma, hmm? Look what Higgins has for you!"

You inch forward as Higgins pours the cream into a rough tin plate. The cat the sailors call Stripes steps out of the gloom to drink. Higgins sighs, "There you go, Momma."

Stripes laps the cream eagerly.

"Who's there?" Higgins gasps. He must have heard your breath.

You step into the light and give your name. "Don't worry. I won't tell."

GO ON TO THE NEXT PAGE.

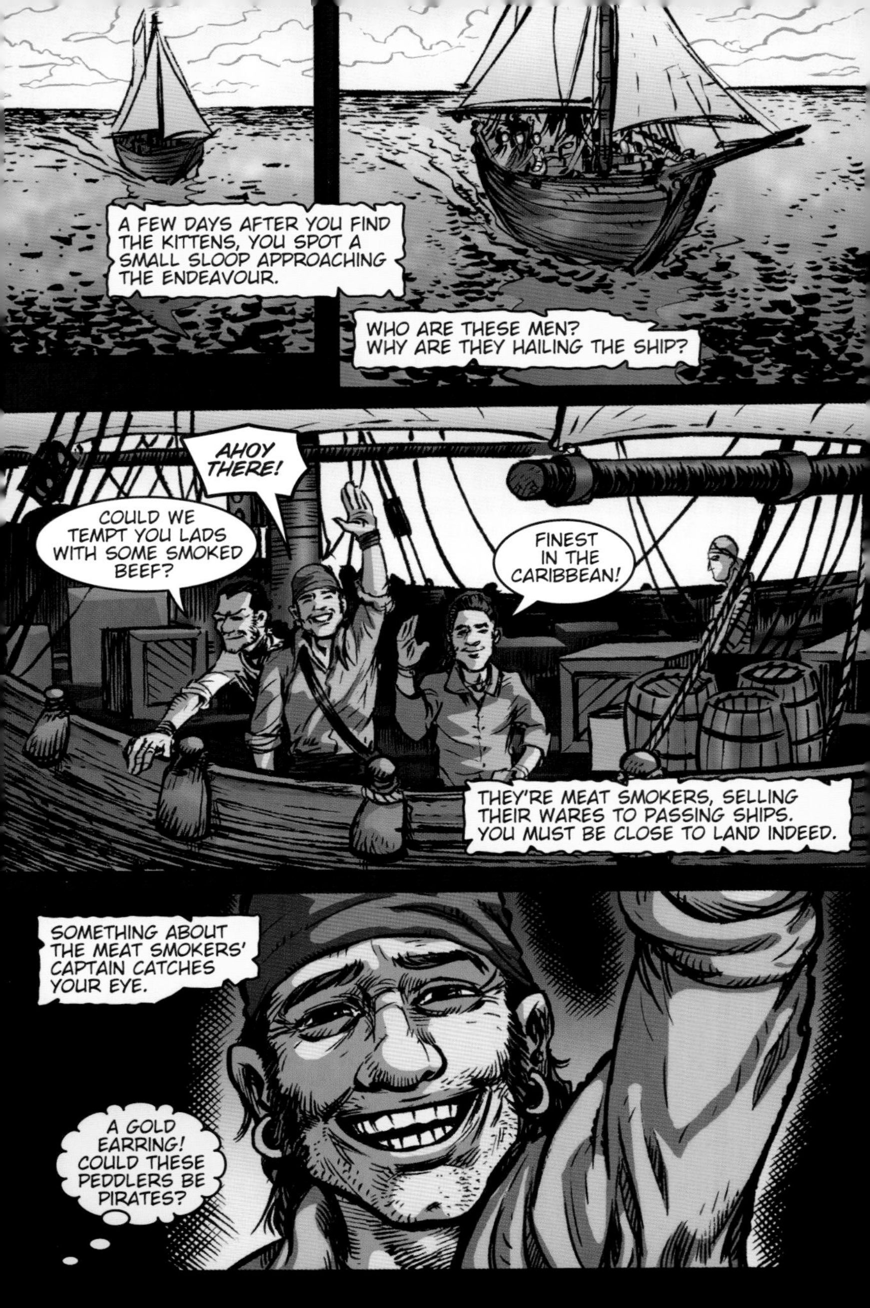
A FEW DAYS AFTER YOU FIND THE KITTENS, YOU SPOT A SMALL SLOOP APPROACHING THE ENDEAVOUR.
WHO ARE THESE MEN? WHY ARE THEY HAILING THE SHIP?
AHOY THERE!
COULD WE TEMPT YOU LADS WITH SOME SMOKED BEEF?
FINEST IN THE CARIBBEAN!
THEY'RE MEAT SMOKERS, SELLING THEIR WARES TO PASSING SHIPS. YOU MUST BE CLOSE TO LAND INDEED.
SOMETHING ABOUT THE MEAT SMOKERS' CAPTAIN CATCHES YOUR EYE.
A GOLD EARRING! COULD THESE PEDDLERS BE PIRATES?

Some of the sailors think the meat smokers might be buccaneers. Were they trying to peek at the *Endeavour*'s defenses? Did they spot the fake gun ports?

At dinner, you ask if the sailors might be right.

Captain Timothy chuckles. "In a way, all meat smokers are buccaneers. *Boucan* is an Arawak Indian word for dried meat. The Arawaks taught sailors and settlers their recipe. The French started calling themselves *boucaniers*. That's buccaneers in English."

"But I thought buccaneers were pirates?"

"After the Spanish attacked their camps, many buccaneers took to the sea for revenge—and loot," Captain Timothy explains.

"Why would the Spanish attack meat smokers?" you ask.

"Anyone who isn't Spanish might help us defeat Spain," he replies.

You taste the delicious beef, then wonder, "How can you be sure those beef smokers aren't the bad kind of buccaneers?"

Father smiles. "That is enough, child."

You decide to keep your mouth shut—except for eating.

TURN TO PAGE 106

WILL YOU...

...let Stripes have her prey? Who are you to tamper with a hungry mother cat with kittens to feed?

TURN TO PAGE 22.

...grab Stripes before she can leap?

TURN TO PAGE 59.

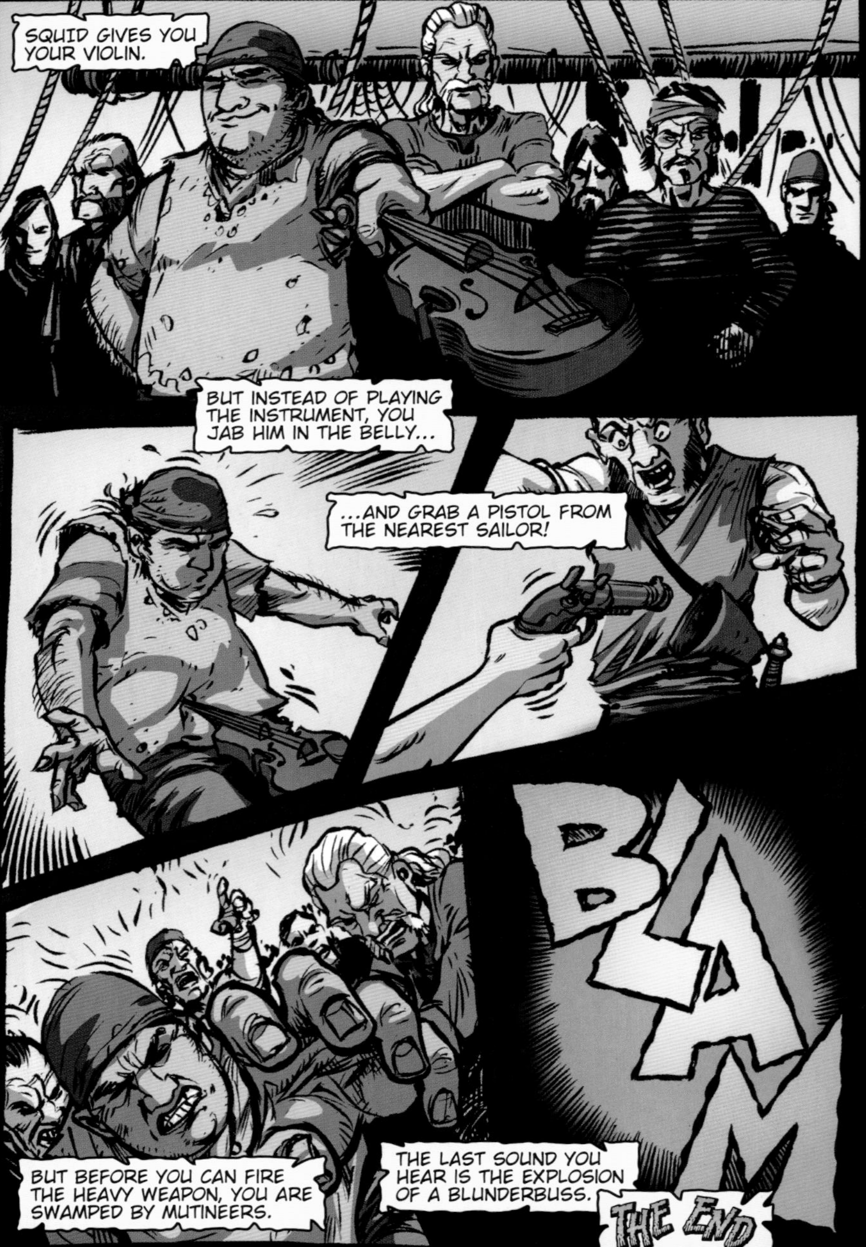
SQUID GIVES YOU YOUR VIOLIN.
BUT INSTEAD OF PLAYING THE INSTRUMENT, YOU JAB HIM IN THE BELLY...
...AND GRAB A PISTOL FROM THE NEAREST SAILOR!
BUT BEFORE YOU CAN FIRE THE HEAVY WEAPON, YOU ARE SWAMPED BY MUTINEERS.
BLAM
THE LAST SOUND YOU HEAR IS THE EXPLOSION OF A BLUNDERBUSS.
THE END

You rush to Father. The pirates allow you to untie the rope that binds him to the mast. "We'll be safe once the ransom is paid, won't we, Father?"

He sighs. "We may not be able to afford the price. I am afraid all our money is invested in this voyage."

Your heart sinks.

"What if we cannot afford the ransom?" another passenger asks.

Captain Jack laughs. "Then you can work like the rest of us—or swim!"

Passengers press gold watches and rings into the pirates' hands.

"Perhaps we can work," you whisper to Father. "At least until we reach a port where we can escape."

"Work for these scum?" Father exclaims.

You cringe, realizing that Captain Jack has heard his remark.

GO ON TO THE NEXT PAGE.

"We are scum?" Captain Jack demands. "We are whatever men like you have made us. You crafty, hen-hearted cheats rob the poor under cover of the law. We plunder the rich armed only with our own courage."

Jack's crew grumbles in agreement. Father looks frightened.

"Men like you drove us to leave our homes and desert our ships in search of a better life. And by the sweat of our backs, we earned it—until the Spanish took it away with their swords," the buccaneer continues.

The pirates clash their cutlasses. One cries out, "Death to the Spanish dogs who killed our mates!"

"Death!" answer the rest.

"If you're too good to work, drown—and your little brat with you!" the Captain concludes.

GO ON TO THE NEXT PAGE.

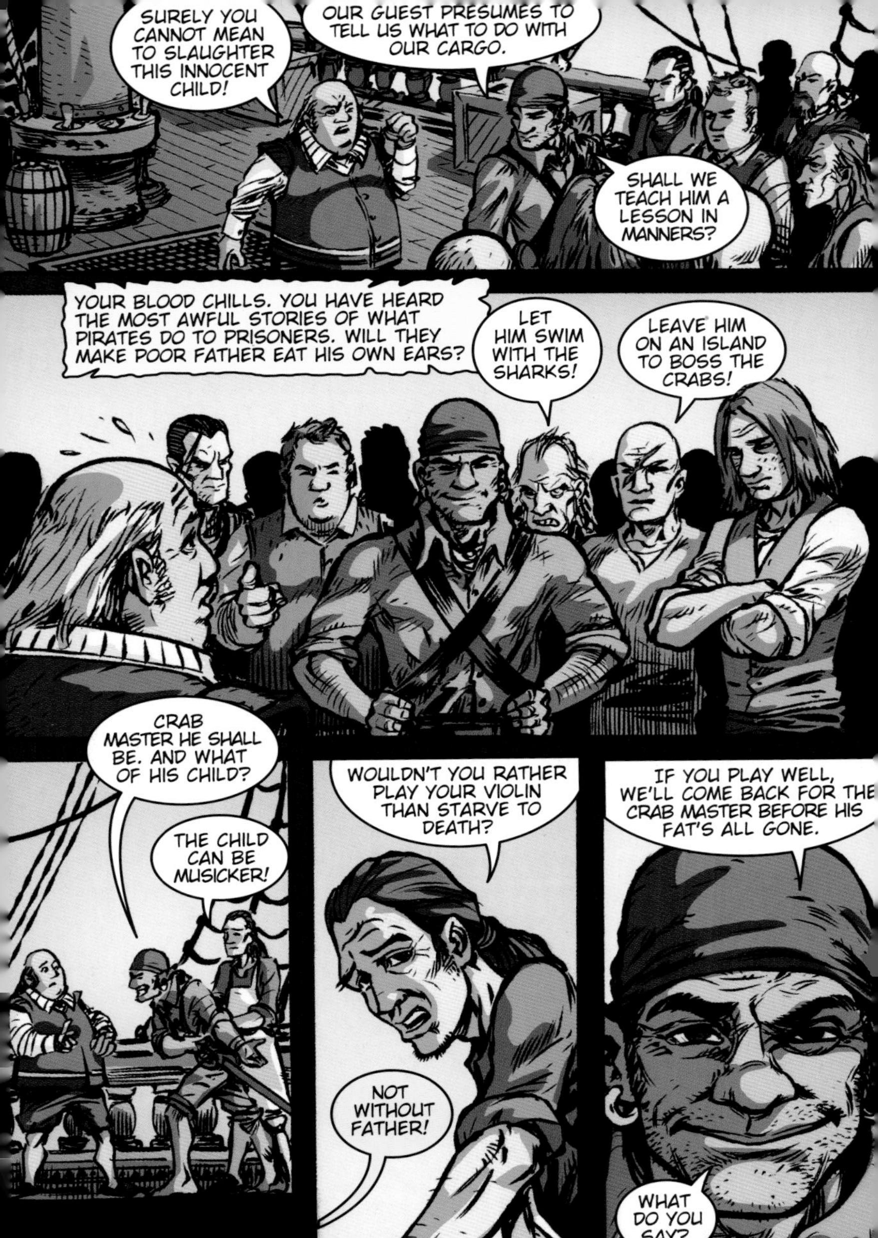
SURELY YOU CANNOT MEAN TO SLAUGHTER THIS INNOCENT CHILD!
OUR GUEST PRESUMES TO TELL US WHAT TO DO WITH OUR CARGO.
SHALL WE TEACH HIM A LESSON IN MANNERS?
YOUR BLOOD CHILLS. YOU HAVE HEARD THE MOST AWFUL STORIES OF WHAT PIRATES DO TO PRISONERS. WILL THEY MAKE POOR FATHER EAT HIS OWN EARS?
LET HIM SWIM WITH THE SHARKS!
LEAVE HIM ON AN ISLAND TO BOSS THE CRABS!
CRAB MASTER HE SHALL BE. AND WHAT OF HIS CHILD?
THE CHILD CAN BE MUSICKER!
WOULDN'T YOU RATHER PLAY YOUR VIOLIN THAN STARVE TO DEATH?
NOT WITHOUT FATHER!
IF YOU PLAY WELL, WE'LL COME BACK FOR THE CRAB MASTER BEFORE HIS FAT'S ALL GONE.
WHAT DO YOU SAY?

TURN TO PAGE 26

After dinner you can't stop thinking about buccaneers.

WILL YOU . . .

. . . have a heart-to-heart talk with Father?
TURN TO PAGE 31.

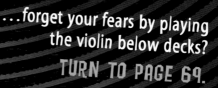

. . . forget your fears by playing
the violin below decks?
TURN TO PAGE 69.

Before the full crew, Higgins is stripped to the waist to be flogged!

"Couldn't he just say he's sorry and promise never to do it again?" you ask.

Father shakes his head. "Discipline must be maintained." But instead of keeping the crew in line, the flogging  fuels their anger. A few days later, Higgins and the other sailors grab weapons and take over the ship. They throw the captain overboard and threaten the same for Father and you. This is a full-scale mutiny!

Then Higgins shouts, "I have a better idea. Flog the tattletale brat!"

Suddenly, you are tied to the rigging. You hear the whip whistle. It lands on your back with a burst of pain as sharp as a knife and hot as a branding iron. Higgins's hysterical laugh is the last sound you hear before you pass out.

THE END

The wound swells and turns black. Long faces and grim muttering reveal that you're doomed. If you only lose the arm, you'll be "lucky."

Smitty says, "I knew a swab once had a wound even blacker than that and they cured it with maggots."

Have your ears and mind gone along with your swollen arm?

Smitty explains, "Flies lay their eggs in dead things. When the maggots hatch, they'll eat away the dead part of your arm. With any luck, you'll be rid of the gangrene."

The disgusting treatment works! Fascinated, you decide to study science when you finally return to England. You become known for your medical discoveries. When you grow old, your grandchildren love hearing about your Caribbean adventure—and the time the baby flies saved your hand. You only wish Father's part of the story had a happier ending.

THE END

You consider how to make best use of the knife.

WILL YOU . . .

...grab the nearest pirate as a hostage?

TURN TO PAGE 17.

...kidnap Captain Jack's navigator to take you to Father's island?

TURN TO PAGE 32.

You find no game, but just enough seafood to fill your growling bellies. One morning, Father stubs his toe on a jagged rock. The wound becomes infected.

In a feverish rant, he says terrible things about himself, you, and even Mother. You tend to him as well as you can. Days later, the fever lessens, but Father is never the same.

One day, a merchant ship passes near. You use the bullets to signal the ship. You are rescued! But the cold, wet weather of home proves too much for Father. Soon you're an orphan.

You join the navy and bury your grief in work. You rise to the rank of admiral, devoting your career to destroying the pirates who ruined your life.

You finally catch up with Smoky Jack and take your revenge. But, of course, this does not bring back Father or your innocence. You will miss both for the rest of your life.

THE END

THE HEAVY PISTOL WOBBLES IN YOUR HAND.

BLAM

YOU MISS!

LITTLE BRAT! THINK OF ME EATING SMOKED BEEF WHILE YOU STARVE!

ENJOY YOUR STAY!

YOU FIND NEITHER FOOD NOR FRESH WATER. THIRST IS A SLOW, TERRIBLE DEATH.

LET US PRAY FOR A MIRACLE.

NO MIRACLE COMES. BUT MADNESS BRINGS YOU RELEASE FROM THE PAIN, UNTIL YOU BOTH PASS INTO THE NEXT WORLD.

THE END

WHICH TWISTED JOURNEYS®
WILL YOU TRY NEXT?

#1 CAPTURED BY PIRATES
A band of scurvy pirates has boarded your ship. Can you keep them from turning you into shark bait?

#2 ESCAPE FROM PYRAMID X
You're on a visit to a pyramid, complete with ancient mummies. But not everything that's ancient is dead . . .

#3 TERROR IN GHOST MANSION
You're trapped in a creepy old house on Halloween with a bunch of spooks. And they aren't wearing costumes . . .

#4 THE TREASURE OF MOUNT FATE
Can you survive the monsters and magic of Mount Fate and bring home its treasure?

#5 NIGHTMARE ON ZOMBIE ISLAND
Legend says no one escapes Zombie Island. Will you be the first? Or will this nightmare be your last?

#6 THE TIME TRAVEL TRAP
Dinosaurs, Wild West train robbers, robots . . . . Danger is everywhere when you're caught in a time machine!